Cold as Thunder

Cold as Thunder

Jerry Apps

The University of Wisconsin Press

Publication of this book has been made possible, in part,
through support from the **Brittingham Trust**.

The University of Wisconsin Press
1930 Monroe Street, 3rd Floor
Madison, Wisconsin 53711-2059
uwpress.wisc.edu

3 Henrietta Street, Covent Garden
London WCE 8LU, United Kingdom
eurospanbookstore.com

Printed in the United States of America

This book may be available in a digital edition.

Library of Congress Cataloging-in-Publication Data

Names: Apps, Jerold W., 1934- author.
Title: Cold as thunder / Jerry Apps.
Description: Madison, Wisconsin: The University of Wisconsin Press, [2018]
Identifiers: LCCN 2017042904 | ISBN 9780299315900 (cloth: alk. paper)
Subjects: | LCGFT: Novels.
Classification: LCC PS3601.P67 C65 2018 | DDC 813/.6—dc23
LC record available at https://lccn.loc.gov/2017042904

For
Steve and *Natasha*

Contents

~~~~~~

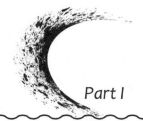

Part I

September, Year Sixteen
of the Eagle Era

One

Andy Schmidt's Solar-Powered Electronic Device (SPED) buzzed. Andy and his wife of two months, Liz Carall-Schmidt, sat under the big pine tree in front of the old farmhouse where Andy had been born. They enjoyed the wonderful smell of the pine tree and the soft sounds the pine needles made when the early evening breeze moved through them. They especially enjoyed the mourning doves that called every evening about this time, the sound rising up from the valley where the Crystal River flowed.

At sixty-three, Andy had thick gray hair, a closely cropped gray beard, and gray eyes set deep within his tanned, wrinkled face. Liz's long, gray hair was tied in back, setting off her round, full face. Her brown eyes lit up when she talked, and her eyebrows lifted when she made a point. Liz was born on the neighboring farm, and she and Andy had been in the same class at Crystal River High School. Both had left their home farms to go off to college. Upon graduation with a degree in agriculture, Andy worked for a time as a university extension agent, but he had returned to the home farm after his father died and he never left again. Liz had been a professor at Badger State University but was forced to return home when her position was eliminated.

Liz and Andy sat here under the big pine tree every evening after they finished work in the big vegetable garden that provided them a modest living. Resting. Talking. Worrying. Hoping. They knew that under the tree the chances that a Social Responsibility drone would hear them was remote, so they talked freely, something they couldn't do out in the open working in their garden or selling their produce at the Crystal River Farmer's Market every Saturday.

It seemed a drone was always present: listening, watching, recording, and sending a stream of messages to the local Office for Social Responsibility (or OSR, as it was often called), where they were reviewed and checked for comments that might indicate terrorist threats as well as for complaints about how difficult times had become since the Eagle Party had come into power sixteen years ago. Mostly the OSR heard few complaints, however, as a broad sweep of the country's population was complacent, hoping that through obedience and hard work, they might join the tiny group of millionaires who lived well and controlled the Eagle Party.

Liz and Andy remembered well the presidential election eighteen years ago, when John Emery of the Eagle Party was elected. In the years leading up to the election, a majority of the people in the country had become totally disillusioned with both the Democratic and Republican parties, and were especially unhappy with Congress, where nothing got done except incessant arguing and backstabbing. Wages for the working class had stagnated, and job opportunities, especially for those with limited education, were becoming increasingly limited. American workers blamed illegal immigrants for their lost jobs and corporations for moving jobs offshore. Congress largely ignored the president's leadership, when he showed some. Many Americans believed that they were taxed too highly and that they received little for the tax money they sent to Washington and to their state governments. They resented too many "lazy people" receiving welfare payments. "Anything is better than what we have now" became the rallying cry for millions of Americans. Out of this mindset of dissatisfaction, John Emery emerged as a representative of the newly formed Eagle Party, promising to "take the dreaded government off the backs of hardworking citizens, provide jobs for everyone, and keep citizens safe from threats within and outside the country."

There were protests at the time, but though the voices were loud, their numbers were small, and they were shouted down and on occasion literally beaten down by those who saw in John Emery and the Eagle Party a new day with a new kind of government. Two years after his election, all levels of government came under Eagle Party control.

Liz and Andy wondered if those who had voted for President Emery and other Eagle Party candidates would have done so if they had known that the Eagle Party would almost immediately vote to abolish the Constitution of the United States and even establish a new calendar, marking their assumption of control of the country as the beginning of the Eagle Era. The Eagle Party withdrew American forces from all worldwide conflicts, not caring about the global ramifications, and turned their focus to domestic issues.

Sixteen years later, American life had drastically changed. In place of the Constitution, the Eagle Party instituted its own moral code, which was strictly enforced by the Offices of Social Responsibility, and began privatizing many aspects of the government. Soon after the Eagle Party gained power, Congress voted to eliminate the dollar as a medium of exchange, replacing it with Eagle credits. Americans did all their financial transactions using Eagle credit cards, drawing on their Eagle accounts, which were kept for them in the National Eagle Bank, with local branches scattered across the country. Those who had things for sale received Eagle credits, as did those who were employed in the various agencies, businesses, and industries.

Only the rich and those working for the Eagle Party could afford electricity these days. The rest relied on lamps and lanterns to light their way. Earlier, Liz had lit the kerosene lamp that sat at the center of their kitchen table, casting a soft, yellow light that spilled out the window to the kitchen porch, and to the bench where Liz and Andy now sat resting and talking under the pine tree.

"Better check my messages," said Andy. He glanced at his government-supplied SPED. "Probably the daily inspirational piece from the *National Eagle Reporter*." The digital *Reporter* shared state and national news, along with so-called Notes of Inspiration. Owned by the New Society Corporation, all information first had to pass by the eyes of the Social Responsibility Truth Squad, which eliminated anything that was remotely critical of the Eagle Party or that might, in some way, upset readers. One-half of 1 percent of all taxes collected went directly to the New Society Corporation to ensure that their efforts were profitable. The internet, once available to all, was now owned by the New Society Corporation, which was closely monitored by the Eagle Party as to what was allowed. All communication between the United States and other countries was conducted only by the Eagle government. No private communication between individuals in the United States and other countries was allowed.

"It's a message from Herman up in Door County," said Andy. Herman Schmidt, two years older than Andy, had left the home farm and moved to Door County when he was thirty years old to work in the shipyards in Sturgeon Bay. It had been a good job until the Eagle Party won nearly all the elections and eliminated minimum-wage laws. He quit when his hourly pay dropped to five Eagle credits per hour, the equivalent of five dollars an hour. Now Herman lived on a couple of acres near Baileys Harbor, where he grew vegetables and strawberries that he sold to visitors in the area. His garden also provided him enough food to tide him over winter.

Andy quickly read the message: *Dear Andy, Kind of nice here. Interesting tourists. Lazy days. Listening to the birds. Energizing time. Relaxing. Soothing place. Taking it easy now. Otherwise, nothing new. Ran a mile today. Maybe tomorrow, too. Herman.*

"Something's wrong," said Andy. He tried to remember the code that he and his brother had established to exchange messages with each other. "Let's see," Andy said. "If Herman includes 'Dear' rather than just 'Andy,' he's sending a secret message. And if he signs it 'Herman' rather than just 'Herm,' it means the message is the first letter of the first word in each sentence." Andy translated and said the coded message aloud, "Killer Storm."

It hadn't rained in Door County since April, and then only a quarter of an inch. Not even the old-timers remembered such a hot, dry summer. For the last ten days the temperature had climbed above 100 degrees each day—unheard of in Door County, which was known for its moderate temperatures, cooled by Lake Michigan on the east side of the peninsula and the waters of Green Bay on the west. The golf course grasses crunched underfoot and even watering—long since banned by the local Office for Social Responsibility—wouldn't have kept them green.

"Oscar, do you see what I see on the radar?" asked Josh Winkler.

As head meteorologist for the Northeast Wisconsin Weather Company, Oscar Adams was responsible for predicting day-to-day weather throughout northeastern Wisconsin. Since the Eagle Party had eliminated the National Weather Bureau, all weather forecasting had been turned over to private companies. These for-profit weather companies provided detailed forecasts to farmers, cranberry growers, tourist attractions, ski hill operators, and others who depended on accurate weather information for their success, and were willing to pay for the weather information.

The weather companies also had responsibility for broadcasting storm warnings on the Eagle Network—serious thunderstorms, threats of high winds, and possible flooding from heavy rains. These warnings would appear on all SPED communication devices. In a serious weather emergency, the companies could also use broadcast drones to get out the message.

"I see it," answered Oscar.

"This looks like the big one," said Josh. "Same storm that hit the east coast yesterday. Killed a bunch of people. Flooded out more of New York City. You gonna let the local OSR know?"

"Have to. If we wanna keep our license to operate we gotta let those folks know about any serious storms. And this one looks like a doozy." Oscar quickly sent the following message:

Powerful Storm predicted to hit Door County in twenty-four hours. Permission requested to broadcast the following warning:

High Wind and Flood Warning

Winds exceeding 200 miles per hour will arrive in northern Door County and slowly sweep south toward the city of Green Bay by tomorrow. It is strongly recommended that anyone living in Door County, especially in low-lying areas, should evacuate. A storm surge of at least 25 feet is predicted from the waters of both Green Bay and Lake Michigan. Rain to exceed 10 inches each day for three days is expected. Severe property damage is predicted with extensive flooding. Downed trees. Trailer courts demolished. Many homes and other buildings likely to be destroyed. Washington Island residents should immediately leave the island, as it will likely be completely flooded.

Mae Fitzgerald, head of the local Office for Social Responsibility, received the urgent message on her computer, but she was not at her desk. As was her custom, every morning from nine until ten, she drank coffee in the cafeteria with several of her coworkers.

When she returned to her office and sorted through her messages, Oscar's finally caught her attention. Rather than immediately give permission to the Northeast Wisconsin Weather Company to broadcast the warning, she thought it best to contact her supervisor, Fred Putkey, state director of the Office for Social Responsibility in Milwaukee.

High Priority

Received this urgent email from the weather company in Green Bay. Please advise.

Mae Fitzgerald, Local Director

Fitzgerald received an immediate reply.

To: Mae Fitzgerald.
From: Fred Putkey, Director, Wisconsin Office for Social Responsibility.

DENY THE REQUEST TO BROADCAST A STORM WARNING.
REPEAT: DENY THE REQUEST TO BROADCAST A STORM WARNING.
WILL CAUSE PANIC IN DOOR COUNTY.

Fitzgerald immediately forwarded the message to Oscar Adams at the weather company. He couldn't believe the decision.

"Josh, we've gotta warn people," Oscar said to his coworker at the weather office. Within a few seconds the message was on every SPED screen in the county. And within minutes broadcast drones were in the air, flying low over Washington and Rock Island, and then south, zigzagging across the county with their message to evacuate immediately.

"Evacuate. Evacuate. High Winds, drenching rain. Severe flooding."

The warning came too late. Some had noticed the clouds building in the west and felt the breeze pick up. Both those who lived year-round in Door County as well as regular visitors to the county had seen lots of weather come and go, and this seemed like another storm. It wasn't.

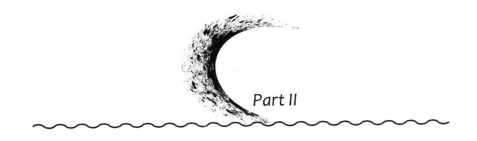

Part II

The Previous May

Two

Patrick O'Malley glanced out the window of the modern, air-conditioned classroom at Crystal River High School, where he was a senior. It was a day in May filled with sunshine and new growth. The school's lawn had greened up, and the oak trees lining the drive to the school had leafed out. The newly installed flower beds sparkled in the mid-morning sunshine. Patrick could see the three flags that flew in front of the school: the US Stars and Stripes on the tallest pole in the center; a bit lower and to the left, the state of Wisconsin's flag; and on the right, the flag of the Eagle Party, depicting a bald eagle in flight clutching a half-dozen arrows in its sharp talons on one foot and a shiny silver coin in the other.

In a few days Patrick's formal education would end and he would join his father at the Crystal River Sawmill, where Aaron O'Malley had worked since he finished his schooling.

Patrick, at eighteen, was six feet tall and broad-shouldered. He had a shock of unruly red hair and green eyes, like his Irish father. Unlike most of his fellow students at Crystal River High, who dropped out when they reached age fifteen, Patrick liked school and convinced his parents that he should stay and graduate, even if the expense was sometimes more than the family could bear. When the Eagle Party took over the public schools in year three and sold them to the highest bidder, all schools, from elementary through high school, became for-profit institutions where the students' families covered all costs for attending. Even though the schools were privately owned institutions, the government still required that each of them adhere to the Eagle Party's values, which included personal responsibility, self-reliance, respect for authority, and the importance of competition and winning at all cost.

Patrick especially enjoyed his English courses and had become a good writer. Occasionally his English teacher, Molly Mason, criticized his writing, not for its technical qualities but for the topics he chose to write about. She cautioned him about dwelling in areas outside the scope of the assignments. Patrick wrote an essay raising questions about whether it was healthy for the United States to have essentially just one political party, the Eagle Party. Molly Mason liked Patrick, and after he had turned in the controversial piece, she took him aside after class. "I won't report you to the Office for Social Responsibility," she said. "I'm supposed to report any student not adhering to party principles. So watch it." She smiled when she said it, touching Patrick on the arm. She had told him that one of her friends, a fellow English teacher at another school, lost his teaching license for sending a less-than-flattering message about the party to another teacher, who turned him in for the "defamatory comments."

The National Eagle Educational Corporation of New York had purchased the Crystal River High School building and began operating it as a for-profit institution with a vastly revised and "improved" curriculum focusing on preparing young people for the world of work and emphasizing moral values in all aspects of life. The curriculum, now identical at all high schools in the United States, was formulated by a special education committee of the Eagle Party to ensure that the same values were taught throughout the country so, in the party's words, "the country could return to its former greatness when competition and individual initiative were applauded and people knew how to lead moral lives."

The local Offices for Social Responsibility made certain that the curriculum offered at all schools did not run contrary to the Eagle Party's beliefs and values. Schools were first and foremost designed to prepare students for the workforce. Students must learn discipline, punctuality, patience, how to follow directions, and that they must not at any time question authority. They must learn that those in authority must be respected and revered. The elementary and high school curriculum focused on reading, basic writing, practical mathematics, and a few other required courses.

Most science was considered a hoax, especially if it contradicted the Eagle Party's ideology. Climate change research had been widespread and well supported in the years before the Eagle Party took over the government, but now a teacher who so much as mentioned climate change could be jailed. Classes in sex education were banned. Any instructor who taught critical thinking skills would immediately be fired.

All forms of art education such as music, painting, creative writing, pottery, and drama were deemed frivolous and had been eliminated long ago. Football and basketball, on the other hand, were revered, as these sports were considered to foster the values of taking orders and learning to win at all costs.

There were no elective classes. With every student taking the same courses, employers knew what to expect from the workers when they were hired. Included in the required course list were "The History and Philosophy of the Eagle Party" and "Toward a Moral Life." Both had beginning to advanced versions and were offered to students every year they attended school.

Franchisees of the National Eagle Educational Corporation, a stock company with an annual multibillion-Eagle-credit profit, were required to adhere to the curriculum and to the basic rules and regulations set down by the Eagle Party. The local units of the Office for Social Responsibility enforced the rules. However, the school's franchisee could set its own tuition levels, charge additional fees for sports events, and do what was otherwise necessary to make a profit.

Individual schools within the five regions of the country—Northeast, Northwest, Southeast, Southwest, and Midwest—competed with one another on student achievement scores as measured by monthly tests that each student was required to take in all subjects. Franchise owners of elementary and high schools in each region with the top test scores were invited to Washington once a year to meet with the president and receive gold medals and national publicity. The Midwest region had won this prestigious award the previous two years.

With advances in technology, students at all levels received a minimum of half their instruction online through their SPEDs. The Eagle Party, using tax funds, provided SPEDs to every person aged five and older. The national office of the Eagle Educational Corporation prepared the online instruction for students, with guidance from the national Office for Social Responsibility. With online teaching available, students were required to attend classes at the schools on Mondays, Wednesdays, and Fridays only. On Tuesdays and Thursdays, the schools were used for worker-training programs of various types, depending on the businesses and industries in the community.

Teachers were usually the lowest-paid citizens in the community—and the profession, if it could still be called that—was generally held in low esteem. Because teachers only worked three days a week, most supplemented their income with part-time jobs as they could find them.

Many taxpayers were thrilled when the public school became for-profit institutions. They saw their tax bills fall to levels they had never known. Of course parents now had to pay the tuition and fees for their children to attend school—and all children had to attend until age fifteen. If a family with children in school neglected to pay the required per-student tuition, the tuition charges made their way to the family's yearly tax payment. The vast majority of the students dropped out of school at age fifteen and went directly into the workforce as common laborers. The graduation rate at the rural high schools was about 20 percent. In the cities, the graduation rate hung around 10 percent, sometimes even lower.

The Eagle Party wasn't concerned about these low graduation rates, as its members had long warned against an overeducated workforce. With too much education, workers began asking questions, and sometimes even challenged orders given by their supervisors. Even worse, an occasional worker might suggest how to improve the work setting or make it safer. Such suggestions were out of line. Workers needed enough training (the party did not use the word "education") to do their jobs, and no more.

Patrick and the eight other students in his senior class—there had been thirty-five students when he enrolled as a freshman—sat in the nearly empty study hall. Patrick paged through *A Guide for a Moral Society*, a well-worn copy with a leather cover that he had been given when he was ten, and that he must carry with him at all times. Like his fellow seniors, he was required to read and memorize large portions of the *Guide* as part of his coursework.

As he sat in the study hall, he read yet again the list of guidelines for how to live a moral life, and thereby become part of a moral society.

Personal success is measured by wealth.

Avoid joining groups—they sap the energy from individual achievement.

If you are not a winner, you are a loser.

Avoid thinking; it gets in the way of productivity.

Do not trust the work of science and scientists.

Never question authority; respect it.

Hard workers do not need excuses.

The greatest friend you have is yourself.

Winning is everything.

Immigration should be stopped.

The environment and its resources are there for your use.

"We have a great hope," Patrick's instructor and high school principal, Sylvester Hightree, had recently said, "that one day the entire world will accept and applaud the writings in *A Guide for a Moral Society*." Hightree had gone on to point out, "Since the Eagle Party has come into power, Morals have once more returned to the classroom, and our once-great country can move steadily forward as our founding fathers had intended."

Now Patrick saw the study hall door open and watched Principal Hightree enter the room. Hightree, resembling his name, was six feet five inches tall, thin as a red pine, and so strict that when he entered a room one could not hear a piece of paper rustle. Everyone in the high school, freshmen through seniors, was required to attend the Wednesday afternoon Social Responsibility Seminar, which Hightree led. Patrick had attended these sessions every week since he was a freshman, and with each session he was increasingly bored. He wanted to ask questions about many of the statements and guidelines in this supposedly infallible book. He wanted to go beyond it and even, perhaps, go in a direction different from what the "never to be questioned" book was proclaiming as the perfect society.

When the hour-long discussion was completed, mostly a one-way lecture from the principal, Hightree stopped by Patrick's desk, put his hand on Patrick's shoulder, handed him a big brown envelope, and whispered, "Do not open this until you arrive home." Then Hightree quickly turned and left the room.

Three

Does the 'bugmeister' have anything to report?" asked Liz Carall. Liz served as president of the Crystal River Oldsters, a group of about forty retired people in the community, who were mostly former educators. There were also a couple of nurses, two medical doctors, two building contractors, and several former business owners. Additionally, Pastor Larry Williams belonged to the group. He had been a longtime pastor before the Eagle Party came into power and banned all churches and all forms of religion and absolutely forbid the use of the word "God" in any way.

"Whether people know it or not, spirituality is an essential part of people being human," Pastor Larry said often. Beyond this group of Oldsters, he dared not express his thoughts and feelings for fear of being jailed or worse.

Oldster members had to be sixty years old to join and had to have their application approved by a majority of the members. The group met weekly in what had once been the community room of the Crystal River Library. The Eagle Party had closed all libraries and this building became the Last Chapter Saloon.

"I've disconnected the listening bug—as per our usual protocol," reported John Owens, a former physics teacher who had taught at Crystal River schools. Bald, short, and full of energy, John was responsible for disabling the always-present listening device during their meetings and reconnecting it afterward. The group hoped those responsible for listening to the hundreds of listening devices the Office for Social Responsibility placed throughout the community wouldn't notice an hour's lapse in communication from the bug at the Last Chapter Saloon.

After the members finished lunch and made sure all the doors were closed and Bill, the bartender, was not in the room—the OSR had informants everywhere—Liz turned to Andy Schmidt and asked, "Do you have an updated garden report?"

"I do," said Andy, who grew and donated most of the flowers—petunias, geraniums, marigolds, asters, and several more varieties—that Oldster volunteers planted around the city. By planting and caring for flowers throughout the Crystal River community, the Oldsters stayed in the good graces of the local OSR, which was generally concerned about any group meeting. The Oldsters claimed to buy the flowers at a distant greenhouse—and in fact did buy a few of them there, in case someone from the Office for Social Responsibility would take time to check.

"The flowers planted near the high school are doing well, as are the ones in front of the OSR building and in front of the Eagle Industries factory."

"Any problems?"

"I could use a few more volunteers to help with weeding—weeds always seem to grow better than the flowers."

Several hands went up, and Andy noted the names in a little notepad he always carried.

"Thank you," he said.

"And now to memorabilia sales," Liz said and turned to Emily Taylor, a former English teacher at Crystal River High School. Emily, who had never married, was sixty-one but looked forty. She was slim, athletic, and had an ever-present smile.

"Yes, memorabilia sales," said Emily. The group ostensibly used profits from sales of memorabilia produced by the local Eagle Industries factory to finance their community beautification project, but everyone in the Oldsters group knew that the funds earned from selling "Eagle Party junk," as some members described the goods, had a far more important purpose. Emily adjusted her glasses and began her report. "So far this spring, our sales have been outstanding. Wealthy folks from Milwaukee and Chicago passing through our beautiful little village generally stop at our Oldsters kiosk on

Main Street. Here is what has sold best in recent months: caps, T-shirts, sweatshirts, stuffed eagles, coasters, tapestries, pillows, and playing cards. The three books that the publishing unit of Eagle Industries produces also sell well: *The Eagle Story* for kids, *The History of the Eagle Party*, and not to forget the famous *Guide for a Moral Society*. As we all well know, everyone over the age of ten is required to have the *Guide* with them at all times," she said with a sneer, and held up her well-worn copy to show that she complied. "Our funds are in good shape."

"That's what I wanted to hear," said Liz, smiling. But the smile quickly turned to a frown as she continued. "I hate to have to say this, but our movement appears to be stalled. We meet every week, we talk, we get emotional about what must be done—yet little is changing. If anything, the educational system in this country has gotten worse in the last few years—if that could be possible. If you don't have sufficient Eagle credits, the police won't answer your call, nor will you have access to medical services. Our roads are terrible, and we can hardly breathe without the Office for Social Responsibility knowing about it. No one seems to care about the environment, the ever-increasing pollution of our streams and groundwater, and even worse, people are ignoring the inevitable effects of climate change that are surely here."

Heads were nodding in agreement.

"Education is one way out of the mess this country is in," said Liz. "And what do we see coming out of these for-profit schools? Children who have been indoctrinated in the ways of the Eagle Party. Children who have never known a real education. Children who have been trained to be machines like the ones they will operate when they leave school. Children who have no opportunity to think on their own, and who are punished when they do. We've made some progress with our scholarships to Onthaway Academy. But what else can we do?" Liz looked around the room.

"Let me begin," said Emily. "We surely must keep providing scholarships to Onthaway in Canada. As you all know, at Onthaway we are developing a cadre of people who are trained in a broad approach to education. When we teach there for those few weeks each summer, Liz, John, and I see students who are learning to use education as a way toward social change, learning about the importance of respecting the environment, learning that water is sacred and must be treated as such. Learning that we must change our ways of living to slow down climate change. But we've got to do more."

"What do you suggest?" asked Andy.

"Let me back up a little," said Emily. "Onthaway Academy has been in operation for five years, but only one in fifty schools has a teacher who has attended the training camp. There is little these teachers can do by themselves to change the direction of the curriculum and the teaching strategies without getting caught, fired, or even jailed. We've got to figure out a way for our Oldster chapters—we've got about fifty of them now in Wisconsin—to do more to help these young teachers who are committed to teaching such things as critical thinking, creativity, appreciation for the arts, leadership development, evolution, and environmental protection— topics that we used to teach but have since been outlawed by the present administration."

"Here's a thought," offered Liz. "I suggest we start planning this summer for an underground student movement in the high schools, led by the graduates of Onthaway and supported by Oldster chapters."

"Isn't that a little dangerous?" piped up John Owens.

"Of course, but the very fact that our group meets every week is dangerous."

"How would we begin such an effort?" asked Emily.

"Some of you know Molly Mason, who started teaching English at Crystal River High last year. She attended Onthaway two years ago and is undercover as one of our Oldster Associates. I suggest we make our relation-ship to Molly more public. Let's invite her to come to our meetings as a liaison member—a conduit to the school. I don't think the OSR would have a problem with that. In fact they'll applaud us for reaching out to the school—they've been encouraging Oldster chapters to work with the schools in just this way."

"But isn't that just so we can help sell parents on the idea that the schools are accomplishing a lot and keeping the kids on the straight and narrow?" Andy pointed out.

"Absolutely. But that doesn't mean we can't use their system to our advantage," Liz replied.

Oldster chapters throughout the country were encouraged to enlist elementary and high school teachers as Oldster Associates so the Oldsters had firsthand information about happenings in the schools. The information presented by the administrators often avoided telling the truth and indeed seldom included what was really happening. Most often they presented a rosy picture of student accomplishments that far exceeded reality. Because parents were required to pay tuition for their elementary and high school students, it was important that parents remained satisfied with the school's accomplishments.

"I move that we invite Molly Mason to become a liaison member of the Crystal River Oldsters," offered John.

"Second," said Andy.

Four

When Andy returned home from the Oldster meeting, he walked out to his big garden, grabbed his hoe, and worked his way to the end of one of the long rows of vegetables. On this May day, the potatoes, radishes, lettuce, and broccoli were already fighting with the emerging weeds for sunlight and moisture, while other vegetables were yet to be planted—the beans and the squash and the pumpkins. He sat down on a weathered wooden bench he had placed on the end of the garden several years ago. The day was warm and sunny, and it was generally pleasant to be outside in the fresh, clean air—well, mostly clean air. When the wind was in the right direction, he could smell the mega dairy farm located several miles away, on the other side of Crystal River. He could also often smell the huge hog farm, which was even closer.

Andy had grown up on this farm. His father before him had been a dairy farmer, growing vegetables that he sold at the farmer's market in Crystal River to earn a little extra money.

Upon graduating from Crystal River High, Andy received a scholarship to attend Badger State University in Madison, where he studied agricultural education. He had known he was fortunate; few students had the opportunity to attend a university at that time. After earning his degree at Badger State, he accepted a job as a university extension agent in Brown County. He was one of a cadre of extension agents working in every county in

Wisconsin, employed jointly by the federal government, Badger State University, and the county. His job had been part of what was called the Wisconsin Idea, a philosophy that proclaimed that the boundaries of the university were the boundaries of the state. Andy carried the results of research, developed at the university's research farms and laboratories, directly to the farmers of Brown County. He loved the work and enjoyed the satisfaction he got from helping farmers and their families improve their farms, increase their incomes, and enjoy a better way of life. But after five years, Andy got a call from his mother saying that his father had died. Andy made a difficult choice. He resigned his position and returned to the home farm and never left again.

Andy, a bit weary from hoeing the weeds, sat on an old, gray bench—a simple, angular style known as an Aldo Leopold bench, named for the Wisconsin conservationist who designed it long ago. Andy thought, *No one knows anymore about Aldo Leopold, who proclaimed the need for people to live in community with the land. No one seems to recognize that we all have a responsibility to take care of the land, to cherish it, and do whatever we can to assure that future generations will benefit from our work. Today ever-increasing global warming is threatening the planet. No one dare even mention it. If the words "global warming" or "climate change" are spoken today, they set off a fury of reprisals from the ever-present Office for Social Responsibility.*

He remembered his father saying, "These times are cold as thunder," when he described hard times on the farm—when crop prices were low, when they were stuck in a long drought or some other calamity befell them. But even these cold-as-thunder times bore little resemblance to what had been happening since the Eagle Party had taken over the country. Power and accumulated wealth were driving everything, the environment be damned and climate change be ignored.

Sometimes Andy discussed Leopold and even climate change with his special friend and neighbor, Liz Carall, who had been born and raised on a farm only a skip and a jump, as people used to say, from Andy's home farm. Liz agreed with him about many things, but they disagreed as to what problems should top the list of concerns. Andy felt climate change was the biggest threat. Liz argued that education was of equal concern. And education to her mind was the only way to confront climate change.

Andy looked at his SPED and scrolled through his messages, but he saw nothing of importance beyond the daily Note of Inspiration from the federal OSR in Washington. Today's message read: *Hard workers do not need excuses to excel.* He laughed when he read it. He had worked hard all his life and what had it gotten him? Not much, barely enough to survive. *Unfortunately*, thought Andy, *so many people believed that if they worked hard they would one day join that small group of multimillionaires who were running the country these days.* He laughed again at the thought.

Andy pushed his SPED back into his pocket and grabbed his hoe. He had been hoping for a text message from Liz. After Andy's wife died, he became a lonely man, working these acres with essentially no one to talk to. But since Liz had moved back to her home farm, all that had changed. Liz had made life bearable for Andy.

And lately, once or twice a week, Liz spent the night with Andy, breaking every moral rule in the Eagle Party's *Guide for a Moral Society*.

Five

Liz Carall sat in her little office in the old farmhouse where she had grown up, looking at the wall where she had hung her diplomas: bachelor of science, master of science, PhD, all earned at Badger State University.

Cradling a cup of tea in her hands, she considered the framed diplomas, reminders of an earlier day, a better day, when academic achievement was a badge of honor, not a curse. She had worked hard to earn these degrees, as her farmer parents had little money to support her academic work.

She smiled as she remembered the day after she completed her PhD, when the head of the Department of Environment and Society, Dr. Joseph Baxter, her major professor, asked if she would consider an assistant professor position in the department to teach and continue her doctoral research. *What a wonderful feeling to be selected for that prestigious position*, Liz thought. *To be an assistant professor in a department that only a few years earlier had been rated the best Environment and Society Department in the United States.*

She took a long sip of tea and recalled the first research proposal she submitted to the world-renowned Gold Brothers Foundation in New York City. She remembered the proposal title, how could she forget, as it had become the theme for her many years of research at Badger State University: *New Strategies for Environment and Society Education.*

Some years later, she received a grant for two million dollars from the

Foundation for the Environment and Society. With that research funding, she had been able to advance her theories about environmental education as a way to revitalize societies. Her teaching, research, and outreach work and her writings took her to groups throughout Wisconsin, where she shared her research. She was promoted to associate professor with tenure in six years, and when she became a full professor, three years later, she published *Foundations for Environment and Society Education*, which became a *New York Times* best-selling book.

With the book well received, she was soon on a speaking circuit talking to groups throughout the United States and in several foreign countries in addition to her teaching and research responsibilities at Badger State. Liz recalled the talks she gave in places like Buffalo after a fierce snowstorm; Phoenix, where it was so hot the airplanes wouldn't fly; and Anchorage, where her host's son was prevented from playing soccer because they couldn't encourage a moose to leave the soccer field. She recalled the time she lectured in The Hague, with the angry waters of the North Sea pounding the sea wall a few hundred yards from the conference hotel, and she recalled the lecture she gave in Jackson, Alberta, with the mountains in the background and elk eating grass on the hotel lawn.

Liz recalled the spirited discussions that followed her lectures as people debated and raised their voices when they differed on the basic question of how lifelong environmental learning could contribute to a revitalized and sustainable society. The debates became even more robust when people differed on what the basic characteristics of that society should be. There were always some who believed everything was just fine the way it was: "Everyone knows that you can't do anything about the environment, especially about the weather. And this business about climate change—well that's a hoax university researchers came up with years ago so they could get more research money."

But Liz was convinced that the scientific evidence about climate change was accurate. She also believed that environmental education, at all levels, from preschool to older adults, could provide long-range answers to help deal with the problems threatening the environment and the planet's supply of clean water.

For Liz, her work was continually challenging and rewarding, and she felt that she was making an important contribution to Wisconsin, the rest of the country, and indeed the world.

But then, budget cuts had led to the elimination of many environmental education programs, especially hands-on, field-based programs. To add to the challenges, several states eliminated teacher and public-employee unions. As a result of that action, teachers lost much of their prestige as leaders in society.

As Liz remembered, *If there was ever a time the United States needed leaders to examine the ways by which lifelong environmental learning could revitalize a stagnant society, this was the time.*

She and her research team at Badger State University had been prepared to help. She believed her research results suggested clear, doable strategies to illustrate the importance of environmental education and why it was essential for—she dared not even say it—the survival of many communities. She drafted a long letter and sent copies to several national legislative leaders offering her assistance—to speak to groups, conduct workshops, and help with local research projects. She received no replies. Not one.

For a time, Liz continued to receive limited research funding from national educational and environmental foundations for her studies. She advised her graduate students and continued to teach undergraduate- and graduate-level courses on the importance of environmental education and its role in society. She continued writing for newspapers and magazines as well as for academic journals. She was a popular speaker at national and international environmental conferences.

Liz never would have believed that any political party would eliminate all public education, but the Eagle Party quickly did. Within three years of assuming power, the Eagle Party had converted all public elementary and secondary schools in the United States to for-profit institutions with identical curricula, all designed to prepare young people for the world of work and little more. There was no longer any mention of nature or the environment in any school curriculum.

As a tenured professor, Liz had been protected for a while, and although the topics she spoke and wrote about had become increasingly unpopular with the majority of voters, she continued on. *I know that what I was doing was important*, thought Liz as she poured herself another cup of tea. *But I should have seen it coming that higher education would be next on the list to feel the wrath of the Eagle Party.*

Liz never forgot the day. She was speaking at the University of Michigan to a packed lecture hall of faculty and students. She was asked to do a two-hour presentation, with a break after the first hour. After a few words of introduction, Liz turned on her laptop computer and the following appeared on the big screen behind her:

Challenges to Environmental Education

Several generations with no direct contact with nature
Ignorance of people's relationship to the environment
Relationship to nature viewed as purely economic
Environmental regulations believed to destroy jobs
Misunderstanding of science and scientific research
Exploitation of natural resources
Everything judged according to its monetary value
If you can't measure something, it doesn't exist
Focus on today: the future is someone else's problem
Parochial view of people's relationship to the world

She carefully discussed each point, illustrating how these personal beliefs and values had become the predominant ones in today's society. An hour had already passed when Liz glanced at a clock. "Whoops," she said. "I promised you a break and I have already gone past my first hour. See you back here in twenty minutes."

Liz took out her smartphone and checked her email. Topping the list was a message from the president of Badger State University. She had never received correspondence directly from him before. Liz thought little of Oscar Oliver Prescott; she was put off by his pompous use of three names, and in his capacity as an administrator, she believed he had sold out to the Eagle Party–controlled legislature. She read:

Dear Faculty Member:

By legislative action and the governor's signed approval, Badger State University will see significant changes in the years ahead. At this time, no one should be unduly upset, especially those faculty with strong, nationally funded research programs.

The following adjustments will take place:

1. All teaching activities at this university will cease as of September 1. This includes all undergraduate as well as graduate classes.
2. All outreach activities not directly in support of a faculty member's research program will cease.
3. Tenure is abolished. Faculty will work on a year-to-year contract basis.
4. Faculty research will focus on practical research, especially that which relates to job creation and the enhancement of for-profit business activities.
5. All faculty members' proposed research must be reviewed and approved by a committee consisting of Badger State University administrative officials and governor-appointed business leaders.
6. Faculty members who wish to continue their present research programs must submit requests to this office for administrative consideration on or before July 15 of this year.

Sincerely,
Oscar Oliver Prescott, PhD
President, Badger State University

As Liz thought back to that day in Ann Arbor and the news that would change her life, she took another sip of tea and put down a print copy of the email, which she had just taken out of her desk drawer to reread once again. She remembered how she and her research team had spent several weeks writing and rewriting the research statement that she would submit to President Prescott's office. She was certain that her national reputation as a leader in environmental education and societal revitalization would allow her to keep developing her several theories and test her action strategies.

Now she looked again at the email she had received two weeks after submitting her letter.

Dear Professor Carall,

We have read your recent proposal with considerable interest but are sorry to say your ideas are outside of our state's research needs. We do not see how your suggestions will create more jobs or enhance the state's business community.

Because Badger State University is now entirely a research institution with no teaching responsibilities, and because your research does not fit our new mission, your services are no longer needed.

Your termination date will be September 1.

Thank you for your previous contributions to Badger State University.

Sincerely,
Oscar Oliver Prescott, PhD
President, Badger State University

After reading the emails, Liz felt a sick feeling in her stomach. She couldn't believe it then and she still couldn't believe it now. She remembered the heart-rending experience of telling her research team the news that they were all out of work.

At the time, Liz had thought about seeking employment in another state, but she was well aware that what was happening in Wisconsin was happening throughout the country. Former major research and teaching universities were being turned into research and development centers for the country's big businesses.

So single, and with only modest savings but in good health, Liz decided to move back to the family farm—and try to figure out what to do with the rest of her life. Never had she felt so angry and depressed. She had, with her parents' support, worked hard to achieve her academic degrees. She had put her heart and soul into academic work as a university teacher and researcher. She had willingly shared her research findings across the country and around the world. And then, like a piece of garbage destined for a landfill, she was tossed aside, dismissed as someone irrelevant, out-of-date, and no longer needed. She had never gotten over that cloud of worthlessness that had become a part of her life when she was fired from the institution she so dearly loved, parted from the work that she knew in her heart was not only relevant but *essential* for society and the country to survive. Being a professor had not only been her work; it had also been her life. She remembered how Andy described low points in his life as *cold as thunder*. This time was clearly a cold-as-thunder time for her.

Liz returned to the farm where she grew up with the hope that her deep feeling of worthlessness would disappear and become a distant memory. But the feeling did not leave. Not a day went by that she didn't think about what could have happened—in her mind should have happened—if she had been allowed to continue her work.

Her spirits were lifted with the buzzing of her SPED. The message was from her neighbor, Andy Schmidt, whom she had known since they were children.

It contained but one word:

Tonight?

Six

Patrick was more than a little curious about the envelope he had stuffed into his backpack as he hurried along the streets of Crystal River, with their fine old oaks and lilacs in full blossom, offering a sweet smell of spring. He passed several Oldster-planted flower beds, but he noticed none of this as he walked toward home—his mind was filled with thoughts of what was in the envelope that seemed to be burning a hole in his backpack. During four years at Crystal River High, he had never received a message from the principal's office.

Was he being expelled from school for his writings? Had Miss Mason turned him in after all? Had Principal Hightree decided that Patrick's questions in a recent Social Responsibility Seminar had been so off base that punishment was in order? But if that were true, why make the information secret? When other students had been caught for breaking one of the hundreds of school rules, they were publically reprimanded. This strategy was very effective, as few students in recent years had broken any rules and most had, as the administration hoped, become docile learners, soon to be docile workers.

Along with his interest in writing, Patrick had developed a keen interest in history, especially Wisconsin history and the history of Crystal River. Oftentimes when he was walking home, he thought about the Native American people who had first lived here. He remembered much of the history of Crystal River that he had read in a book his father had hidden from the Great Collection.

Patrick knew that Crystal River had been founded in 1853 by Welsh and Irish immigrants and for many years was a farming community that first relied on wheat growing and then switched to dairy farming. As he continued on home, he thought about Crystal River today. Today the town had a population of about two thousand people and was home to three major employers. Crystal River Woodworks employed upward of 150 people when times were good. The company included a sawmill and log cabin manufacturing plant, a hardwood flooring operation, and a cabinet unit that made upscale oak cabinets for the housing industry. Eagle Industries was where young men and women unable to find other work helped manufacture memorabilia and published books for the Eagle Party, which many people bought to show their patriotism and love for the Eagle Party. Eagle Industries, which paid its one hundred workers about three Eagle credits an hour, manufactured caps, T-shirts, sweatshirts, and much more, all featuring the big flying eagle with its talons clutching arrows and a silver coin, and emblazoned with the words "The Eagle Party of the People, for the People." The Shady Hill Nursing Home was the third major employer in town, with about twenty people on staff and about 150 residents.

The Crystal River ran through town and through the length of the former Pioneer State Park, some five hundred acres of prairie and woods. Patrick recalled the park's big headquarters building, which included the offices for the park rangers and a huge room with a fireplace at one end, where up to one hundred people could gather on a rainy day. He remembered the good times he had had there with his parents when he was a little kid. The park, just a mile out of town, had been a popular place for everyone to visit back then. Patrick had loved fishing and wading in the clear blue river. Now he couldn't remember the last time he had visited the park, though he passed by its entrance often on his bike. The Eagle Party had put all the parks up for sale to the highest bidder in year seven. A New York investment company purchased Pioneer State Park and renamed it Happy Valley Park. They were more interested in profits than in providing a special experience for visitors. The company had immediately raised the entrance fees to a level that only the rich in the community could afford.

It wasn't long before the state park was privatized that the Great Collection took place. In year six, every citizen in the country had been required to turn in all their books to central collection points where local officials would decide which books would be burned and which books citizens would be allowed to keep. Patrick, then eight, heard his dad tell his mother, "I don't trust those people, I'm gonna keep most of my books. I'll hide them." But most citizens, loyal to the party that they had elected, turned in their books. As Patrick's dad feared, all were burned.

"We're doing this for the future of the country," party officials had said when they were questioned by some people, mainly librarians and a smattering of politicians who had once been active in the now essentially extinct Democratic and Republican parties.

The local Office for Social Responsibility invited everyone to the day of the book burning, which they called "A celebration to cleanse our society of wrongheaded thinking and immoral references." The event was held in the beautiful Crystal River Park through which the Crystal River flowed. The Office for Social Responsibility provided free grilled bratwurst, ice cream, and soft drinks. They hired an accordion player to play patriotic songs as book after book was tossed into the blazing fire.

Directed by the officers of the OSR, the citizens of Crystal River tossed books into the fire. OSR staff carted in loads of books they had collected from citizens who were unable to attend this celebratory event—a celebration for some, a deplorable event for others.

As young Patrick watched the flames lick at the books, he felt sad, for he loved books, and now all that was left of them was a cloud of gray smoke and a pile of ashes. He couldn't understand why this was happening and tried to ask his father, who told him to keep quiet.

An OSR officer came up to Patrick with a copy of *Charlotte's Web*.

"Here, young man, here's a book for you to toss into the fire."

Patrick looked at his father, wondering what he should do. *Charlotte's Web* was one of Patrick's favorite books.

"Do it," Patrick's father said, and the boy tossed the book into the flames to be consumed with the others. Patrick tried to hold back his tears. He couldn't understand why this was happening.

The law required libraries and schools to turn in all their books as well.

Patrick remembered a few days after the big community book burning when he was walking past the public library, one of his favorite places. He saw the librarian, Miss Mary, standing in front of the door with her arms extended as six men pushing a cart filled with books moved toward her. A seventh man walked up to her and said, "Remove yourself woman or suffer the consequences."

"I will not," said the defiant Miss Mary.

The man grabbed her, spun her around, put her arms behind her back, handcuffed her, and dragged her to a big black car parked nearby.

"Save our library. Save our library," Miss Mary screamed as she was pushed into the car. The small crowd that had gathered did nothing. Miss Mary was never seen again. Soon after the Great Collection, all public libraries closed. The Crystal River library building was turned into the Last Chapter Saloon.

As Patrick continued making his way toward home he heard a loud humming sound he recognized as one of the many surveillance drones that regularly flew over Crystal River, as they did over every other city and town. The drones were capable of recording both audio and video. Most people applauded the government's use of drones, for the government regularly reminded them, "The drones are here to keep you comfortable and secure, as they will immediately spot any hint of terrorism or citizen wrongdoing."

Patrick thought about his father, Aaron, and his mother, Barbara, who had both scraped together all their savings to keep Patrick in high school past age fifteen. His father worked in the sawmill at Crystal River Wood-works and his mother at the Sandy Hill Nursing Home.

Patrick worried about his father, especially since he lost a finger in a sawmill accident. Patrick remembered when his father came home from the mill that day, his hand wrapped in his bloody shirt and his finger left in a pile of sawdust at the mill. With no health insurance, the family simply couldn't afford to see a doctor. They called on Patrick's grandfather Sean.

Patrick still had nightmares about what had happened next. The evening of the accident, his father sat at the kitchen table, bloody towels wrapped around the stump of his finger, dark red blood dripping into a pail. Patrick's mother ran down the street to Patrick's grandfather's house, a few blocks away. After she blurted out the details of the tragedy, Sean O'Malley gathered up a few items and followed her home.

When he arrived at Patrick's house, he immediately instructed Barbara to stoke up the wood-burning cookstove. Grandpa Sean placed one end of a steel rod into the flames, and as he waited for the metal to heat, he poured a glass of whiskey from a flask he produced from his coat pocket.

"Drink this," he instructed, thrusting it at Patrick's father, who sat white-faced at the table. When the glass of whiskey was empty, Sean re-filled it and once more Aaron drank all of it, his face turning red and the pain from his severed finger somewhat subsiding.

Sean inspected the metal rod; the flames from the woodstove had turned it from a dull gray to a cherry red. Grandpa Sean grabbed a nearby towel, wrapped it several times around the cool end of the rod, and pulled it from the flames.

"Hold out your hand," Sean instructed, "and look the other way."

Without a moment's hesitation, Sean pushed the burning hot rod firmly against the stump of the severed finger. Patrick's father screamed with a cry Patrick had never heard before as the smell of burning flesh filled the room. The bloody stump, now cauterized, ceased bleeding.

"Oh, oh . . . ," Patrick's father moaned as he slumped back in his chair, nearly losing consciousness.

"Did you have to do that?" yelled Patrick's mother. "Did you have to burn his hand?"

"It's the only way to stop the bleeding," Grandpa Sean quietly said. "In a few days he'll feel better."

"What if someone heard and called it in?" Patrick asked. "What if the police come?"

"The police won't come. We haven't paid our police protection fees this year. No police will come, even if someone heard your dad's scream," said Patrick's mother.

The details of his father's accident were seared in Patrick's memory. He never forgot the sight and smell of burning flesh and his father's agonizing scream. When his father returned to work, he quickly discovered that he could no longer meet the production quotas that were set for every worker. The annual week of unpaid vacation time was no more. Patrick's father worked every day, Monday through Saturday, twelve months of the year. He also was required to attend the worker skill-updating workshops once a month at the high school, on Tuesdays and Thursdays, the days when the regular students were working on their SPEDs at home.

Patrick wondered if his father would be fired as his ability to meet production quotas decreased. He was glad he was completing high school because his family would no longer have to pay high school tuition.

Patrick remembered the time of the accident like it was yesterday, because it was then that his father, who had from time to time questioned the many policies and rules set down by the Eagle Party, essentially gave up. Any fight that he had left had disappeared when he lost his finger. Both Patrick's mother and father had read to him when he was a little boy, and then when he was older, they introduced him to the books that his father had hidden from the Great Collection. When he finished a book, his father would ask him what the book was about, what his thoughts were about what he had read, and what lessons he learned from reading the book. So even though teaching critical thinking was banned in the schools, Patrick was learning how to do it at home.

Finally arriving home, Patrick pulled back a chair from the well-worn wooden table and sat down. He removed the envelope from his backpack. There was nothing especially unusual about it, although he saw few envelopes these days. All the post offices had been closed for several years, and all communication was via email or with text messages on the SPEDs that everyone carried.

Patrick reached in his pocket for his folding knife, which he always carried with him. It had been a long time since he had opened an envelope and he wondered what was so important that he should receive one. With one sweep of his sharp knife, the envelope was open, revealing one sheet of folded paper.

Patrick unfolded it and read:

Dear Mr. Patrick O'Malley:

Upon recommendation of the faculty and a majority vote of Crystal River High School's College Recommending Committee, you are the one student from your graduating class selected to attend Eagle University in Marshfield, Wisconsin.

The provisions of your selection are these:

- By law, unless you have medical reasons, you are required to accept this assignment.
- You have been selected to attend the teacher-preparation thread, and further, your selection includes an emphasis on secondary education.
- Upon successful completion of your degree, you will be assigned to a high school where your services are needed.
- If you fail any of your courses, you will immediately be expelled and sent home.
- You will spend no more than and no less than three years in residence on campus. You will receive two weeks of vacation each of the three summers that you are enrolled.
- All your expenses, including tuition and room and board, will be paid by the university.
- You will be required to live on campus, in quarters provided for students in your major.

Congratulations! Upon graduation from Eagle University, you will become one of a select few young leaders who will help our great country move into the future with the necessary values and beliefs that have made the United States the great country it has been in the past.

It is best that you not boast about this achievement—you will recall from reading *A Guide for a Moral Society*, page 4, "Boasting is reserved only for those who have already achieved great success." And page 5, "Success is measured in monetary worth."

I will send your name, transcripts, and other pertinent materials to Eagle University upon your graduation from Crystal River High School.

Sincerely,
Sylvester Hightree, Principal

Patrick put the letter down on the table and sat back in his chair. He ran his fingers through his red hair. *What does this mean?* he thought. *Is this a good thing? What about all my friends? What will I tell them?* For the last couple of years Patrick had been secretly thinking about one day becoming an official of the Eagle Party. This scholarship to attend Eagle University might be a step in that direction.

He picked up the letter and read it again. His mind was a muddle of thoughts. Just then his mother came through the door, home from a ten-hour shift at the Shady Hill Nursing Home. She was dead tired as usual, but not too tired to notice the concerned look on her son's usually fun-loving face.

"I have news for you, Mom," Patrick said.

Seven

That evening after the Oldster meeting, John Owens took out his SPED, read the daily inspirational message from the Office for Social Responsibility, and then scanned through the digital copy of the *National Eagle Reporter*. Years ago he had been an avid reader of the *Milwaukee Journal Sentinel* as well as the *Wisconsin State Journal*, so he had a good idea of what a newspaper should include. He knew that the *National Eagle Reporter* must be heavily censored for there was never any bad news—no stories of murders, rapes, car accidents, weather-caused tragedies. No letters to the editor. Only good news. Or at least the kind of news that was supposed to make people feel good. *And keep them docile and happy*, thought John.

Just then John's SPED buzzed and he looked at the message. It was from Louie.

The Oldsters communicated with each other in a variety of ways. They often sent text messages on their SPEDs, but they were well aware that the local Office of Social Responsibility monitored all messages so they had learned to use coded messages to send information they didn't want the OSR to know about. They worked hard to keep up their image of being Eagle Party supporters in the hopes that doing so would keep the OSR from paying attention to their digital communication.

According to the Oldsters' rules, John knew that any message from

"Louie" would be a coded message. And when the greeting was "Dear John," he knew that the second letter of the first word in each sentence would form the secret message. With the entire message received, he quickly decoded and wrote down the real message:

O' Malley senior here to U. For O.

Louie

In their various communications, "O" referred to Onthaway Academy, and U referred to Eagle University.

"Louie" was actually Molly Mason, the teacher whom the Oldsters had just been discussing. John Owens was her contact person with the Oldsters, and until the group discussed Molly Mason at their last meeting, he and Liz were the only Oldsters who knew that she was working undercover for them. Secrets remain secrets when few people know them.

In addition to communications via their SPEDs, John and Molly left messages for each other in a hollow tree at the edge of Crystal River Park. John knew that when he received a message of a single word, "yes," and nothing more, he should look for a note in the tree. To the OSR reviewers, the message appeared to be an error—as if someone pushed the Send button too soon.

A few days after the Oldster meeting where they voted to invite Molly Mason to attend some of the Oldster meetings as a liaison to Crystal River High School, John Owens went to the school and met with Principal Hightree.

At the meeting, John said, "Mr. Hightree, we have been impressed with your leadership here at Crystal River High. I come representing the Crystal River Oldsters and we stand ready to help you. You've heard of our group, I assume?"

"Yes, yes, I have," said Hightree. "I know about your efforts in planting flowers around Crystal River. We all appreciate those efforts."

"Well, we want to do more in supporting you and Crystal River High School. To do that, we'd like to invite Molly Mason, one of your teachers, to be a liaison to our group. What do you think?"

Hightree paused for a bit before saying, "I think that would be a great idea. A nice way of tying our school to the greater community. Thank you." He shook John's hand. "It's always great when everyone in the community is on the same page. This seems like one more way to do it. When do the Oldsters meet?"

John shared the meeting schedule.

"I'll talk to Molly and see if she is interested," said Hightree.

"Thank you, Mr. Hightree," John said. He turned and left, smiling to himself.

Of course Hightree knew nothing of what the Oldster chapter had on its agenda, and so far had no reason to suspect that Molly Mason was other than a loyal supporter of the Eagle Party and the curriculum that she was compelled to teach by law.

Molly Mason was twenty-seven and born and raised in Madison. Her parents had been researchers at Badger State University but had been forced out of their teaching roles when BSU became a for-profit research university that no longer taught students. Scientific research that examined basic life forces, the role of stem cells in regenerating human organs, studying the DNA makeup of an organism, or any research related to climate change and global warming were forbidden. However, some of this banned research continued as clever researchers knew how to hide it in what appeared as highly practical and readily applied research—the kind of applied research the Eagle Party wanted, which they believed would create jobs and enhance major businesses.

Charles Mason, Molly's father, was an agronomist who researched drought and hot-weather-tolerant corn varieties. Upon taking over Badger State University, Eagle Party officials and the state Office for Social Responsibility had applauded his work as the ravages of "nonexistent" climate change continued to affect Wisconsin along with much of the country. In some recent growing seasons, Wisconsin had received but a trace of rain in the months of June and July, when normal rainfall would be five or more inches.

Molly's mother, Debra, was a geneticist. She was monitored almost monthly by the Office for Social Responsibility to make sure that her research—which involved splicing genes from one animal species to another—didn't stray into areas where humans were involved. A project she had recently conducted involved splicing genes from a desert lizard into a hog to make the hog more heat tolerant. Climate change resulted not only in periods of both drought and floods but also in extremely high summer temperatures in the Midwest, where moderate temperatures had been the norm for many years.

Molly had attended high school following the prescribed curriculum offered by the Eagle Party. But Molly's parents, like many other BSU professors whose children were forced to attend the for-profit local school, also homeschooled their children, using books they had hidden during the Great Collection.

Thus Molly received a double education—the narrow, politically correct curriculum required by the Eagle Party as well as lessons similar to the education provided in the public schools before the Eagle Party had bulldozed public tax-supported education.

Of course, Principal Hightree knew nothing about these clandestine efforts to educate children, and he had no reason to suspect that Molly Mason was anything other than a supporter of the curriculum, which she was compelled by law to teach. Therefore, when John Owens paid him a call, Hightree was indeed pleased to hear of the Oldsters' interest in happenings at the high school, and he welcomed the idea of Molly become a liaison to the Oldsters' weekly meetings.

Eight

"We have a very special guest with us today," said Liz Carrell after she called the next meeting of the Crystal River Oldsters to order. "We are pleased that she found time in her busy schedule as executive head of our regional Office for Social Responsibility to spend a few minutes with us and bring us up to date on happenings in our region and around the country, especially as they relate to the education of our young people. Let me present Tracy Smith."

After some polite applause, Tracy stood and took her place behind the podium. She wore wire-rimmed glasses and had black hair with a few streaks of gray and a pleasant, friendly looking face with little makeup.

Liz had found out a few things about Tracy from an Oldster from Ohio who had been visiting Crystal River. She learned that Tracy had moved to Wisconsin from Ohio, where she had a role in helping the Eagle Party win the election in that state. Liz learned that Tracy had never married and had spent much of her life in service to the Eagle Party. Being selected as regional head of the OSR in central Wisconsin was likely her payment for her hard work.

"Good afternoon," Tracy began. She had a pleasant speaking voice, not at all the loud, strident voice that was characteristic of so many Eagle Party officials. "First let me say I so much appreciate Liz's kind invitation to speak to you all today."

Several of the Oldsters sat forward in their chairs, wondering what she would say. "I want to commend and thank each of you for your many years of service to your community. I especially want to thank those of you who were teachers. Your work will never be forgotten. Please give yourselves a hand." There was some polite applause, but everyone knew that she, along with most Eagle Party members, believed that former teachers had contributed greatly to the problems the country faced before the Eagle Party took over the reins.

Tracy continued. "I am proud to announce that building on your good work in the past, the Eagle Party has revolutionized education in this country. Let me share several examples."

She paused briefly and sipped from a glass of water, then said, "First, I am pleased to say that employers in this country are elated with the educational system as it has now evolved. Young people are prepared for work. They know how to take orders and know how to respect authority. Their attitude is positive. They are taught these values in our schools."

She once more paused, pushed back a stray piece of gray hair, and continued. "With careful study and research, we've determined that we have spent far too many resources on overeducating our young people. It was not necessary. Good workers do not need excessive education to do their work. This leads me to say an additional important thing. The Eagle Party has determined that paying for a child's education should be the responsibility of the parents of that child, not the taxpayers of the community." She raised her voice a bit. "The Eagle Party has dramatically lowered the taxes for every citizen in this country." She clearly expected applause, and a few Oldsters politely responded, but not many.

"We've made additional progressive changes. We have forbidden the teaching of critical thinking—such thinking is no longer necessary since we have experts in the Eagle Party who think through problems and solutions to problems. We've put values back in the schools, where they belong. We've made sure that no teacher is including any mention of research related to climate change, which everyone knows is a hoax. And finally, our schools are turning out young people with high morals. I'm sure you each own a copy of our popular publication *A Guide for a Moral Society*. Today's students know and follow this guide all hours of the day, both in and out of school. Never in the history of this country have we seen young people with higher morals."

She sipped from her glass of water again and adjusted her glasses. "Do you have any questions?"

Liz held up her hand. "In what way can we help your cause?" she asked.

"Thank you for asking. First, I am pleased that you have agreed to have a liaison person from your local high school who will soon be attending your meetings. I've heard about Molly Mason and the good job she's doing at the school. I also know she will have ideas on how your group can help our cause."

Liz, keeping a straight face, was thinking, *If you only knew why we decided on Molly Mason as a liaison person for our Oldster chapter. If you only knew.* Aloud, Liz said, "Yes, we are impressed with Molly and look forward to working with her."

With that, Tracy moved away from the podium. Liz shook her hand and escorted her to the door.

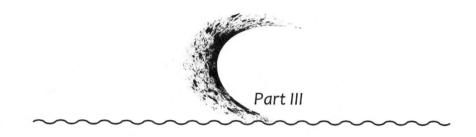

Part III

June

Nine

"You think we've got everything?" Liz asked John Owens as she tightened the straps holding her old, dented seventeen-foot Grumman canoe tied to the roof of her rather ancient Ford car.

"Well, let's see. Sleeping bags. Tents. Some dried food. Cooking gear. Mosquito killer. Water filter. Paddles for the canoe. Flashlights. Backpacks. Think we've got it," answered John.

The time was 7:00 a.m. on a bright and clear early June morning, as Liz, John, and young Patrick O'Malley prepared for their trip to the Boundary Waters Canoe Area Wilderness of Northern Minnesota.

Liz and John made this trip every year for the past several years. This would be the first for Patrick, who had gotten a scholarship from the Oldsters chapter to make the trip. The eighteen-year-old had received the Crystal River Oldsters' annual canoe trip scholarship not long after receiving the letter from Principal Hightree about Eagle University. What he didn't know was that he was being recruited to attend the two-week training session at Onthaway Academy, just across the border in Canada from the Minnesota Boundary Waters canoe area. If he passed muster at Camp Forward, the selection camp, he would move on to Onthaway Academy. If not, he would spend a week canoeing and camping and never know that Onthaway Academy existed.

The threesome traveled north to Eau Claire, then on to Superior, and across the bridge into Duluth, Minnesota. About every fifty miles they stopped and put their Eagle credit card in the tollbooth receptacles owned by an assortment of highway travel companies. They finally arrived in Grand Marais, Minnesota, and pulled in at the Grand National Ranger Station, operated by the Grand National Nature Company, with headquarters in New York City. Grand National had purchased several of the former national parks, including the Boundary Waters when it had come up for sale in year seven.

After paying their camping fees, they turned onto the old Gun Flint Trail that led to the Boundary Waters. Liz remembered when the road was hard surfaced and well maintained, but now it had returned to a rough, rutted, dirt-and-gravel narrow trail. The tolls did not earn enough to provide good roads and at the same time offer a profit to the company that owned it.

Liz drove along the Gunflint Trail more than fifty miles, finally arriving at Camp Forward on Sea Gull Lake, where they dropped off Patrick and his gear.

"I'm sure you'll have a great time," Liz said, giving Patrick a big hug.

"I've . . . I've never done this before," Patrick said. "I've never been in a canoe, never slept in a tent."

"Not to worry," said John as he shook Patrick's hand. "You'll do just fine. And have fun."

Patrick of course did not know that Camp Forward screened all possible candidates for the workshop at Onthaway Academy, a few miles to the north in Canada, and easily reached from Camp Forward by canoe.

Liz continued driving a bit farther on, and then she and John put the canoe into Sea Gull Lake and shifted their camping gear from the car to their canoe. With Liz in the front, and John in the back, they paddled off with their goal the Canadian side of Saganaga Lake and Onthaway Academy, where they would spend the next two weeks teaching.

As Liz dipped the old wooden canoe paddle into the clear water, she immediately began to relax. *How long will these waters remain this way?* she wondered. She had read messages from Oldsters living in Minnesota saying that the Grand National Nature Company was considering leasing a large section of the Boundary Waters to an international mining company.

How many more years will we be able to do this? There's always the possibility that the Eagle Party will find out what we are doing and throw us all in jail or worse. Or the mining company will spoil this area so no one will want to come here.

But as she paddled, she enjoyed the quiet. There were no buzzing drones—perhaps the area was just too large for the Eagle Party to devote much drone surveillance. Besides, few people lived there year-round.

A loon call interrupted Liz's thoughts. John pointed his paddle toward the lone loon, swimming a hundred or so yards to the right of the slowly moving canoe. Its prehistoric call echoed across the quiet lake.

Rounding a bend in the lake, they spotted the familiar portage trail that would lead them to the next lake. Liz pulled the canoe up on shore and she and then John crawled out, stretched, and began unloading the gear from the canoe. Liz slipped on the heavy backpack. Meanwhile, John tipped the canoe over, lifted one end, then stepped under it and adjusted the eighty-pound canoe's portage pads on his shoulders. The two of them trudged off along the portage path, through the woods, John first with the canoe, followed by Liz, with the heavy pack.

After more paddling and more portaging, they finally arrived at Saganaga Lake. They had paddled several hundred yards when they saw a boat with an outboard motor roaring toward them. Quickly they identified it as one of the US Homeland Security boats that patrolled these waters to make sure no Canadians entered the country illegally. They also tried to prevent people from the US sneaking into Canada. The boat was black with white letters that boldly stated US Department of Homeland Security, with the Eagle symbol prominently displayed. The three men in the boat were dressed in black and each carried an automatic weapon.

Liz and John immediately stopped paddling and began digging out their identification cards and their camping permits. The wake of the powerboat rocked the canoe as the inspectors drew alongside, their automatic weapons at the ready.

"Identification, please," the man in the front of the boat demanded. He was in his midthirties, tall and slim. The two canoeists passed their IDs and their camping permits to the man, who carefully looked at them, comparing the photographs with the occupants of the canoe.

"Where will you be camping this evening?" the big man asked.

Liz, not expecting this question, said, "We hope on the south end of this lake, on the US side, of course."

While Liz was talking to the leader of the group, the other two men visually inspected their camping gear in the canoe. Out of the corner of her eye, Liz watched them, hoping they wouldn't open the backpack, for in it she had teaching notes she planned to use in her workshop at Onthaway Academy—notes about how to do creative and critical thinking and strategies for creating a social revolution in the US. She tried to remain calm. Finally after several trying minutes, the big man said, "Everything seems to be in order; you are free to paddle on. We'll stop by your camp this evening to make sure you are all okay. Have a good day." The boat turned and roared off.

"First time that's happened," said Liz. She let out a deep breath. "When I heard that Homeland Security was stepping up their border patrols, I thought they meant the Mexican border, not the Canadian border. Looks like we'll be arriving a day late at Onthaway Academy."

They paddled toward the south end of the lake and proceeded to set up camp. In the early evening, the big black powerboat roared past their camp. They waved at the men in the boat. The men didn't wave back.

Ten

"Welcome to Camp Forward," the thirtysomething woman said as she extended her hand to Patrick O'Malley. "I'm Fred, really Frederica, but everyone calls me Fred," she said.

"Hi," was all Patrick could think to say. He was overwhelmed at the place where he found himself. Like almost all young people his age, he had never left his home community since the Eagle Party came into power. Once they dropped out or finished high school, they immediately went to work for one of the employers in the community. Patrick had never been more than five miles from Crystal River.

"You're Patrick, right?" Fred asked. She wore no makeup and had a friendly smile. She had on a floppy hat, a long-sleeve tan shirt, matching long trousers, and hiking boots.

"Yes, yes, I am," said Patrick.

"Where are you from?"

"I . . . I'm from Crystal River, Wisconsin."

"And where would that be?"

Patrick laughed. "In central Wisconsin, a long ways from here—we drove all day to get here."

"Well, follow me. We'll find a spot for your tent and help you set it up," directed Fred.

Patrick shouldered his backpack, which contained his tent, sleeping bag, and other camping gear, and followed the young woman a few hundred yards up a trail to an open place in the woods. Patrick noticed several other tents already erected in the area.

He had never camped before, never slept in a tent, never been in a canoe. Everything was new to him—not only the sights he saw like the thick woods that surrounded the camping area and the blue water lake just down the hill but also the wonderful, clean smells of the wilderness. He thought of the smells back home in Crystal River—depending on the direction of the wind, you got either the stench of hog manure from the mega hog farm or the smell of cow manure from the huge dairy located just out of town.

Just then a loon called.

"What's that?" Patrick asked.

"A loon. We've got several of them living on our lake. Wonderful sound, isn't it?"

"Never heard it before."

A minute later, Patrick asked, "Are there bears here?" When he had told one of his friends that he had gotten a scholarship to spend two weeks in the Boundary Waters of northern Minnesota, all the friend could think to say was, "They've got bears there and they eat people."

"A few," Fred said, smiling.

"Do they eat people?" Patrick asked, a concerned look on his face.

"No, these are black bears and they don't eat people. They'd rather eat berries," she said, laughing. "Here, hold this." She handed him one end of the tent.

In a few minutes, Patrick's tent was erected, his sleeping bag inside and unrolled along with his backpack, which contained a couple changes of clothing.

"Come with me, Patrick," said Fred. "I want you to meet some of your fellow campers."

They walked toward the lake, where a small cluster of people was gathered around a smoky campfire.

"I'd like you all to meet Patrick from Wisconsin," Fred announced.

The others, all about Patrick's age, said their names: Paul, George, Karen, and Judy.

"Hi," said Patrick, making a small wave with his hand.

"Now that you're all here, welcome to Camp Forward," Fred said. She had blank journals and waterproof pens that she passed around to each camper. "While you are at Camp Forward, I'd like you to record your experiences here—what you liked, what you didn't like, what you learned—that sort of thing."

Patrick looked at his new journal and the shiny pen. He had never had a journal—in fact, journals at Crystal River High were forbidden.

Fred continued. "We have a few rules you must follow. Some of you may be worried about bears. Yes, we have a few bears that are always looking for a handout. Rule number one: No food in the tents, nothing. No candy bars. No trail mix. Nothing. Bears like that stuff. After every meal, our food goes in this canvas food bag, and we pull it up in that big white pine tree, where the bears can't get at it." She pointed to the food bag that was swinging gently in the breeze.

"About the weather. We have some fierce thunderstorms up here. Make sure that all your tent stakes are firmly in the ground so you'll remain dry. A tent properly erected can take quite a beating from the rain and wind."

As Patrick carefully listened to these rules, he began to wonder if he had made the right decision to accept the scholarship to this wilderness place. At home there were no bears and he slept in a house with little chance of it blowing down in a fierce thunderstorm.

"Oh, and you are all expected to help prepare the meals and clean up after each meal," Fred said.

With the talk about food and meals, Patrick realized how hungry he was. He held up his hand. "What time is supper?" he asked.

Fred laughed. "As soon as we can get it ready. Someone go let down the food bag from the pine tree and we'll get supper started."

After supper and cleanup, the little group gathered around the campfire, watching the sunset and seeing the first wisps of fog gather across the cool waters of the lake.

"One of the purposes of Camp Forward is to help each of you learn a little more about yourself, as well as develop confidence in your abilities," Fred said. Patrick didn't quite understand what Fred meant by these words, but he looked forward to the next day. He especially was interested in learning how to paddle a canoe. Soon after he crawled into his tent and zipped up his sleeping bag, he was sound asleep.

Patrick woke to loon calls. He sleepily crawled out of his tent and shuffled over to the campfire, where Fred sat on a log drinking a cup of freshly made coffee.

"Good morning, Patrick," she said, smiling broadly.

"Mornin'," Patrick mumbled as he took a seat on the log.

Slowly, the other campers joined Fred and Patrick. They all sat quietly, watching the mists rise from the lake and listening to a loon that they could see swimming a couple of hundred yards out in the glassy smooth waters of the lake.

After a quick breakfast of oatmeal and dried fruit, Patrick hoisted the food bag high up in the pine tree. He then helped with the general camp cleanup. Soon the group gathered at the water, where three canoes with paddles and life vests waited. Fred pushed one of the canoes into the water, climbed in, and began to demonstrate how to use a paddle, showing the different strokes.

"The person in the back steers the canoe," she explained. She demonstrated the J-stroke as a way to keep the canoe moving straight without shifting the paddle from one side to the other.

"The person in the front helps with the paddling and keeps an eye out for rocks and other obstructions that a canoe can hit and be damaged or even overturned."

Soon the campers were all in canoes, taking turns sitting in the front and back and learning the basics of maneuvering from here to there. At first, every canoe zigged and zagged, but after an hour or so of practice, they all moved mostly in a straight line.

In addition to teaching the basics of canoeing, Fred was mentally noting how quickly each camper caught on to what she was teaching, as well as how each was able to work cooperatively with the person on the other end of the canoe. Frederica Anderson, Camp Forward director, was a physical education teacher in a Duluth high school, and each summer she secretly worked for the Oldsters organization. She had special training in selecting campers who would make good candidates for the Onthaway program. After several years of directing Camp Forward, she saw an uncanny relationship between canoeing and the ability to be flexible in dealing with new ideas and easily working as part of a team, as well as demonstrating leadership potential—all valuable characteristics for those who would benefit most from the Onthaway Academy experience.

After a lunch of cheese sandwiches and trail mix, Fred demonstrated how to build a campfire with one match. She gathered several small pieces of birch bark from a tree that had fallen near camp, along with several small twigs and a few larger pieces of dry wood. With her jackknife, she cut several small ribbons of birch bark and placed them in a little pile. Then she built a little teepee-like structure of small twigs around the birch bark, followed by a few larger pieces. She struck a match, one of the large "farmer-type" matches, and touched the flame to a piece of protruding birch bark. In a few seconds flames emerged from the teepee as the small twigs caught fire and then the larger ones. The campfire was born.

She asked each camper to demonstrate what she had just done. All eventually did it, though Paul and Karen had difficulty building the little teepee of twigs, and thus their campfires sputtered for a bit before taking off as the others had done.

Next Fred showed campers several skills for surviving in the wilderness with minimum preparation, including the proper use of a knife, which wild plants and berries were edible and which were not, how to build an emergency shelter using a blanket, how to find bait for fishing, and how to prepare a fish over an open fire. She spent several minutes discussing emergency shelters as she knew, thanks to her hidden weather radio, that strong thunderstorms were predicted for later that evening.

Before supper Fred told the group, "For the next two days, you will each do something special. I call this your personal quest. You'll have an opportunity to practice what you've learned this afternoon. And you'll probably learn a great deal about yourself."

Patrick and his fellow campers looked at each other, each of them wondering if they were ready for this kind of experience.

"Here's how it works." She handed each camper a little packet. "In each packet there are three matches, a folding knife, a length of fishline with a hook, a canteen of water, and a waterproof blanket. The packet also includes a satellite emergency clip that you can wear. If at any time you don't feel safe or believe you are in an emergency situation, just push this little red button and I'll be alerted and will come to where you are. It may take a few minutes, but I'll be there, no matter what time, day or night.

"Be sure to take your journals with you and write about what you are experiencing and your reactions and feelings. Any questions?"

"What about bears?" asked Karen, looking concerned.

"Won't be a problem. You won't have any extra food for a bear," Fred answered.

"Oh," is all Karen could think to say.

The group ate an early supper. After cleanup, Fred loaded the campers one by one into her canoe, paddling them each to a spot not far from the main camp. The individual campsites could not be seen from each other. Each campsite was high on the bank of the lake and included a clearing with a place for a campfire and little more.

When Patrick arrived at his personal quest site, he saw a bank of clouds building in the west. Although Fred had not mentioned the possibility of a storm, he had learned from his father that clouds like those he was seeing this early evening would likely mean rain. Patrick immediately began looking for a shelter. Not far away he found a recently downed tree and underneath it a place to stay dry in case he was right about the coming storm.

He returned to his campsite and gazed at the lake, which had not a ripple, as there was no wind, not even a typical early evening breeze. He watched as the setting sun slowly moved toward the bank of clouds. He began writing in his journal.

> I don't know what the night will bring, but I am all alone in this beautiful but more than a little scary place, all by myself. No tent. No sleeping bag. Only a thin survival blanket, which looks like it might be waterproof. It better be, because a big storm is brewing in the west. I just saw the first flash of lightning. Those clouds look mean.

He closed the journal and slipped it into the pocket of his jeans. It was becoming too dark to write. He heard a loon call in the distance. It echoed across the quiet waters of the lake, a mournful sound. He thought of his parents back in Crystal River and wondered what they were doing—they had a hard life and now, with his scholarship to attend Wisconsin's Eagle

University in Marshfield, he had the opportunity to become a teacher. No cost to his parents. All paid for by the Eagle Party. Clearly, he would be indebted to the Eagle Party for the opportunity.

He continued looking across the quiet waters of the lake. There was not a sound. No loon calls. No bird sounds. Nothing. Absolute quiet. Patrick had never experienced such quiet. In Crystal River there was always some sound. Traffic. People talking. Sounds coming from Eagle Industries — "clunk, clunk" — as the various machines worked. And of course there was always the low, occasionally muffled buzzing of the ever-present drones flying overhead, sometimes disguised as birds: robins, blue jays, even crows. *They're always there, looking after us. Protecting us.* That's what the folks from the Office for Social Responsibility answered when someone asked about all the drones, though such questions rarely happened anymore.

Patrick's thoughts were interrupted by a low growl of thunder that started in the growing bank of clouds in the west and then seemed to roll across the lake. It was near dark now, as Patrick saw another flash of lightning tear across the angry black clouds, followed in a few seconds by a louder roar of thunder.

Better find my way back to the downed tree, thought Patrick as the menacing clouds grew ever closer and the lightning ever brighter and the thunder ever louder. With so much lightning, Patrick could easily find his way to the big, downed pine tree. He crawled under it and wrapped the thin, aluminum-faced waterproof blanket around his shoulders as a blast of thunder shook the ground.

Soon the first drops of rain began to fall, big drops that splattered on the bare ground in front of Patrick's makeshift shelter. These drops, when they struck the ground, sent up tiny clouds of dust. He could see this with each flash of lightning. Soon the rain came down in a torrent, and the wind began blowing, sending waves splashing against the rocks along the lake's shore. The tops of the trees began shaking, protesting the storm. Patrick heard a loud crack, then a crashing sound as, he assumed, a branch broke off a tree.

Soon he felt a few drops of rain filtering through the dry branches of the downed tree, but not many, and with the blanket around his shoulders he was dry and quite comfortable. The wind soon subsided and the thunder and lightning ceased as the storm moved east. But the rain continued, now falling straight down and soaking the land, but mostly missing Patrick, who sat huddled under the big, downed pine. The sound of waves pounding against the rocks on the lakeshore continued, a rather pleasant sound. Soon Patrick was asleep.

He was awakened by the sound of a loon calling, and then another loon answering. And for a moment he didn't know where he was. He crawled out from under the big tree and walked the few yards to where he could build a campfire. He saw a bright sun coming up in the east and listened to the raindrops falling from the trees, as a slight breeze blew from the west. He was hungry. He thought about what he had with him: a jackknife, some fishline with a hook, three matches—that was about it. It was time to try to catch a fish.

Patrick had never fished, but he had listened carefully to Fred's instructions. "First," she had said, "you need some bait. Worms or grubs work well as bait, and if you can find an old dead and downed tree, dig under the roots and you may find some worms."

Patrick walked along the lakeshore, searching for a downed tree. He thought of the tree where he had found shelter, but Fred had specifically mentioned dead trees and this one had obviously just recently toppled. He didn't want to wander too far into the woods for fear of getting lost. After walking for a couple hundred yards, he spotted a downed tree that was completely dead.

He began digging and soon found three fat grubs. He walked to the lake, scooped a little indentation in the sand, and placed the grubs there. He took out his jackknife, cut a limb about a half inch in diameter and five feet long from a nearby aspen tree, and tied the fishline to the end of the stick. He threaded one of the grubs on the hook, and tossed it into the lake. The grub had scarcely settled into the water when Patrick felt a tug on the line and pulled out a fat smallmouth bass—the kind of fish Fred said the campers were most likely to catch.

Remembering the instructions Fred had given, he did a passable job cleaning the fish with his jackknife, and carried it to the fire pit. Following Fred's directions, he soon had a campfire going, using a bit more birch bark because all the wood was wet from the heavy rain.

Again remembering the survival skills Fred had taught, Patrick soon had the fish suspended on a little wooden spit he made from the branches of an aspen tree. He fed a small piece of wood into the fire, which sizzled for a moment and then caught. Every few minutes, Patrick turned the cooking fish, the smells making him ever hungrier.

When the fish appeared done—Patrick stuck his jackknife into it to check—he removed it from the flames and allowed it to cool for a few minutes. Then he feasted on freshly roasted fish. Later, in his journal he wrote,

> I've never known fish to taste any better than the one I caught this morning with a fish pole made from an aspen branch and a grub I found under a downed tree as bait. It was juicy, tasted a bit like wood smoke, and was wonderful. What a great place this is, and I really surprised myself. I can find my own food and prepare it, too. I can't wait to tell Mom and Dad about this adventure.

Patrick caught two more fish that day. He had one for lunch and the other for supper. That night there was no rain. He slept under the stars, on a bed of pine boughs that Fred had suggested that he and his fellow campers make. On the morning of the second day, he wrote in his journal,

> I've never seen so many stars. They start at one horizon and they stretch to the other. The sky is filled with stars, some bright, some less so, some that twinkle, others that look like holes in the sky with a bright light shining through.

He ate a portion of fish that he had saved from the previous evening's meal for breakfast. With his fishline he had hung this extra food in a nearby tree so the bears could not get at it. He then sat on the lakeshore, writing in his journal and waiting for Fred to pick him up. He was in no hurry to leave.

Eleven

Arriving back in camp, the group members assembled to discuss their personal quest experiences. Patrick immediately noticed that Paul and Karen were missing, and he asked what had happened to them, wondering if they had been injured or worse during the storm a night ago.

"Paul and Karen found it necessary to leave Camp Forward," Fred explained without elaboration. Later Judy, a friend of Karen's, told Patrick that Karen and Paul had become so disoriented and so uncomfortably wet from the storm that they had punched their emergency buttons, and Fred had picked them up and returned them to the base camp. Apparently Fred had made arrangements for them to be picked up from camp.

"Who wants to share something from their journal?" Fred asked.

Patrick held up his hand. Fred nodded at him and he began.

"This morning I wrote what I'm about to read," Patrick said as he began.

I came to this place fearful of what it would be. I've never been away from home. Never been near a big lake. Never been in a canoe. Never built a campfire. And, I've never been alone for several hours—nearly two days.

I can't say enough about how I feel today—I've caught fish. I cooked fish. I ate fish. I found berries. Sure, I was hungry, but I had something to eat. I now know something about how to take care of myself when conditions aren't the best—caught in a big thunderstorm with a deluge of rain, for instance. Sure, there were times when I was uncomfortable. But life is not always filled with comfortable moments. I learned how to make do when I was uncomfortable.

George and Judy shared entries from their journal with readings similar to Patrick's.

"Excellent," said Fred. "You've all done well, and now I have a surprise for you."

The remaining three campers looked at Fred, wondering what new adventure she had for them. What could be more challenging than several hours alone on a personal quest?

"What I am to tell you is top secret. You must not tell anyone, not even your parents or best friends back home. You must especially keep this secret information about Camp Forward from the Eagle Party's Social Responsibility officials. When people ask what you were doing at Camp Forward, you should tell them you were learning how to canoe, learning survival skills in the wilderness, and having a good time. All true."

Patrick was now more than curious about what Fred was about to share.

Fred continued. "Camp Forward is supported by the Oldster organizations—they paid your way here, as you all know. They wanted you to have a good time, but more importantly, Camp Forward is a place where candidates are selected for Onthaway Academy."

Patrick, now confused, asked, "So what's Onthaway Academy?"

"It's a special place," explained Fred, "where the Oldster organization trains teachers and students who wish to become teachers and leaders in environmental education. The overall purpose of Onthaway Academy is to reestablish in our society the people's concern for the environment, including helping them with strategies to help turn around the environmental destruction that has been occurring since the Eagle Party took office. Ultimately, the goal—to put it bluntly—is to have an educated group of citizens who will vote out the Eagle Party and replace it with an administration that will listen to the will of all the people, not merely the wealthy, and that concern for the environment will be high on their agenda."

"But . . . but," Patrick stammered, "I'm indebted to the Eagle Party. They are paying my way to Eagle University to become a teacher."

"I happen to know that, Patrick, and that's one of the reasons we want you to attend Onthaway Academy. We need people like you in our universities and schools to help make the changes we hope to see happen."

Patrick shook his head, confused with what he was hearing.

"You each have until suppertime to make a decision about whether or not you want to attend Onthaway Academy, which is only a short canoe ride from here, across the Canadian border."

All day Patrick sat thinking about what he should do. He remembered so well how the Eagle Party had treated his father. He couldn't strike from his memory the day his dad lost a finger at work and his family couldn't afford a doctor. He would never forget his father's screams when his grandfather cauterized the cut with a burning hot poker.

He thought about the dull and difficult lives several of his friends lived earning low wages and working hard at the various Eagle-supported businesses and industries, and about the drones that monitored everything he and everyone else in Crystal River did. He remembered well the stories both his mother and his father told him about a better time, when wages were higher, people had health insurance they could afford, and the police and firefighters came without checking to see if you had enough Eagle credits to pay.

But Patrick's mind was a muddle. He couldn't forget that the Eagle Party was paying for him to attend Eagle University and become a teacher. Didn't he have a responsibility to be loyal to them? Did he want to be an undercover agent for the Oldsters—a group he had never guessed was plotting to overthrow the government?

For two hours he sat by the lake, listening to the music of the waves lapping on the rocks that lined the shore, hearing the occasional call of a loon in the distance, and smelling a trickle of smoke from the little campfire that Fred kept burning all day. He thought about his personal quest, and how good he had felt about thinking for himself, figuring out how to solve a problem such as staying dry during a wicked rainstorm. All of this was appealing to him, the more he thought about it. And Fred assured him that after attending Onthaway Academy this year, and perhaps in additional years, he would be able to help others take charge of their lives.

"I'll go," said Patrick when he saw Fred just before supper. Judy and George had made the same decision. After supper and good-byes, Fred gave the three of them a map and the use of one of the canoes. She told them to stick to the shores of the lakes they crossed so the Home Security Patrol would not easily spot them. She waved as they paddled out of sight to the north, on their way to Canada and Onthaway Academy. Fred now had a few days to rest before the next group of potential Onthaway Academy candidates arrived at Camp Forward.

I hope all of this will help make a difference, she thought. *And that we're not putting these wonderful young people in too much danger.*

Twelve

Liz Carall and John Owens broke camp before dawn and quietly loaded their canoe. With Liz paddling in the front and John paddling in the back, they quietly glided toward the Canadian side of Lake Saganaga. This early morning, with the sun not yet up, the lake was covered with mist and fog, making their travel nearly invisible. They didn't want the Homeland Security officers to see them, so they were taking every precaution.

After two hours of paddling, they glimpsed through the mists now lifting from the lake the log cabins and the dining and meeting building of Onthaway Academy. The academy had once been a remote resort owned by the Canadian government, which continued to own the property. For the past several years, it had been leased to the Oldsters at no charge. Indeed, several Canadian environmental leaders had been so upset with the aftermath of the Eagle Party takeover of the US government that they convinced the little-known Canadian Office of International Relations to help fund the operation of the academy. As one Canadian environmental leader said, "When the United States sneezes, Canada catches a cold, and we've been hearing lots of sneezes since the Eagle Party came into power."

Canada provided the director for the academy as well as a maintenance man and a cook. Helgi Ostman, academy director, spotted Liz and John's canoe and waited at the beach for their arrival. When Liz climbed out of the canoe, the six-foot-tall and bearded Ostman engulfed her in a big bear hug.

"So good to see you again, Liz," he said.

"Sorry we're a day late," she replied. "Some of our overzealous Homeland Security men made sure we spent a night camping on the US side of the border."

"I was a bit worried," admitted Ostman.

"So was I. We've never been stopped and inspected like that before."

"Well, that's all in the past. So good to have you on our staff once more," Ostman said.

Liz Carall first met Helgi Ostman at an environment and society conference in Winnipeg, where Ostman was a professor of environment and society education at the University of Manitoba—similar to Liz's position at Badger State University until she was fired. They had been friends ever since even though communication was nearly impossible since the Eagle Party blocked many messages, especially those sent out of the United States.

By this time John Owens had clambered out of the canoe and Ostman greeted him with a vigorous handshake and said, "Glad to have you onboard for another summer, John."

Ostman turned to Liz. "Any new student candidates from Wisconsin?"

"One possibility. His name's Patrick O'Malley. If he made it through Camp Forward, he should be here in a couple of days. There should be others with him from Camp Forward as well."

"Very good!" Ostman said enthusiastically. He knew Frederica at Camp Forward well and had great respect for her ability to sort out candidates for the academy.

"Hans should be here in a few minutes to help with your gear. See you all at the dining hall at lunchtime when we can catch up on what's going on in your lives."

Hans, the academy's maintenance man, arrived with his solar-powered maintenance cart, loaded the twosome and their gear, and deposited each of them at their own little log cabin, each with a view of the lake. The cabins were named after animals. Liz's cabin, the same one she had stayed in every summer, was called Owl. *So appropriate*, thought Liz as she glanced at the name and the wood carving of an owl over the door. *Owls are supposed to be wise, but they also move with little noise and are seldom seen.*

This little log cabin, which included a combination sitting room and mini-kitchen plus a bedroom and bath, would be her home for the next two weeks. She brewed a cup of coffee and walked outside to sit on the little porch that looked out over the lake. She had an hour to herself. The quiet once more engulfed her. All she heard was the slight breeze sifting through the tops of the pine trees and the quiet bubbling of gentle waves caressing the stones along the lakeshore.

She began writing in her journal.

Once more I am at Onthaway Academy in Canada. Such a beautiful place to enjoy and to learn. As I do every year, I wonder what the participants in my workshop will be like this year. I especially worry about the new students that various Oldster chapters have recruited to come here. None of them have known an approach to education different from the one advocated by the National Eagle Educational Corporation. None of them have received any instruction about environmental concerns that face the world. None of them have been exposed to critical thinking approaches or creative thinking activities.

How many of these young people will rebel and push back on what we are doing here? Even with the good work Frederica does at Camp Forward, sometimes I wonder if these young people are so indoctrinated with the Eagle Party philosophy that they will not, indeed cannot, change.

I worry about Patrick O'Malley, assuming he made it through Camp Forward's screening. He's a bright kid—I learned a lot more about him on our long trip from Crystal River. He seems delighted to have received a scholarship to attend Wisconsin's Eagle University, where teachers and business leaders are prepared. But will he be open enough to see that the education he has so far received has been narrow and completely politically motivated?

I guess we'll see, won't we?

The *clang, clang* of the dinner bell on a post near the dining hall announced that lunch was ready. Liz closed her journal and tucked it away in her backpack.

Entering the dining hall, she spotted John and Ostman sitting with someone Liz had not yet met. As she joined them, Ostman said to the little group at the table, "Before we pick up our lunches from the buffet, I want you to meet Otto Gottburg. Otto is an associate professor of climate and weather at the University of Manitoba and has agreed to teach our workshop on climate change, which is his area of research."

Ostman introduced each of them, and Gottburg shook each person's hand. Gottburg, in his midthirties, was close shaven, deeply tanned, with closely cropped blond hair and an easy smile. He had a firm handshake.

"So glad you're with us," said Liz. "We can't even mention the words 'global warming' or 'climate change' in the United States."

"I know," said Gottburg. Trying not to sound critical, he added, "Failing to slow down global warming will be our undoing. If the US doesn't cut back, the whole globe suffers, especially its near neighbors like Canada. The evidence is clear. Becoming clearer every year."

Workshop participants began filtering into the dining hall and lining up at the counter to pick up their noon lunch consisting of salads, make-your-own sandwiches, a chocolate chip cookie, and either cranberry juice or coffee.

Liz looked over the group. All had previously attended the academy, the majority of them as teachers and the rest as college students. The group would grow a bit as those from Camp Forward arrived.

I wonder how all of this will come together this year? thought Liz. *So many changes need to be made in our educational system to include the broader curriculum we are advocating. So many. Can this tiny group make a difference? I keep hoping. But the hill we have to climb is so steep. And there are so many obstacles to overcome.*

Thirteen

Patrick O'Malley paddled in the stern of the borrowed canoe with his new friends. George paddled in the front and Judy, in the middle, read the map that Fred had given them. After several hours of paddling, they arrived safely at the place marked on the map with a red *X*, Onthaway Academy. It was late in the afternoon, and they were hungry and tired, but also thankful they had arrived safely, and successfully avoided being stopped by one of the border patrols. Following Fred's advice, as much as possible they had paddled close to shore to avoid being easily detected.

Hans, the maintenance man, spotted them coming and alerted Helgi Ostman, who greeted them, helped them unload their gear, and instructed Hans to find them beds in one of the bunkhouses where all the participants stayed. "Supper is at six; listen for the dinner bell," Ostman said.

Patrick was nearly overwhelmed with the beauty of the place. At the same time he was more than a little uneasy about what Onthaway Academy was trying to accomplish. Still, once he was settled in the men's bunkhouse, he crawled onto his bed and almost immediately fell asleep. The clanging of the dinner bell awakened him. Soon he was in line waiting to pick up his supper meal. The smell of baked bread filled one end of the dining hall, making Patrick even hungrier.

Liz Carall moved quickly so she was directly behind Patrick in line.

"Hi, Patrick," she said.

Surprised at hearing a familiar voice, Patrick turned to see her smiling face.

"What . . . what are you doing here?" stammered Patrick. "I thought you were canoeing."

"We were, but we were on our way here. I teach here, Patrick."

"You do. You teach here? You are a part of this place? I thought you were an Oldster." Patrick had a confused look on his face.

"I am an Oldster, Patrick. And the Oldsters run this place, with the help of the Canadian government."

"Really," was all Patrick could think to say. They continued toward the meal counter, picked up their trays, selected the food they wanted, and then sat together at a table.

"So how was Camp Forward?" asked Liz between bites of fresh bread.

"Really cool," said Patrick. "Learned a bunch of stuff. How to paddle a canoe. How to build a campfire. How to catch a fish. How to take care of myself in a rainstorm."

"Sounds interesting," said Liz.

"It was. It really was. But what about this place? What's gonna happen here?"

"You'll find out after supper. Director Ostman will go over the plans for the workshop."

"Hi, Patrick." A young woman stopped at their table.

"Miss Mason. What . . . why are you here?"

"Sorry to surprise you, Patrick, but I'm a participant here, just like you. Except I've been here before."

Patrick was putting it all together. "Let's see if I've got this straight. You're a teacher but you are also working undercover for the Oldsters?"

"That's right, Patrick. Welcome to the group," said Molly Mason.

"So that's why you didn't report me to the Social Responsibility Committee when I apparently wrote about things I shouldn't have?" Patrick said, looking at Molly.

"That's right, and I'm also the one who recommended that the Crystal River Oldsters give you a scholarship to Onthaway—but first you had to pass muster at Camp Forward, which you obviously did."

"Wow," Patrick said. He was trying to wrap his mind around all this.

With the meal finished, everyone moved to the back of the dining hall, where chairs were set up.

"Everyone find a seat. please," said Helgi Ostman, "and we'll get started with our orientation. First I want to introduce three new members to our group. They've just arrived from Camp Forward. Stand when I call your names and remain standing until I recognize all of you. Patrick from Wisconsin, George from Minnesota, and Judy from Iowa. A big welcoming round of applause for all three of them."

Loud applause filled the room, even a couple of whistles.

"Now I'd like to introduce your instructors for this year's workshops. Two have been here before, one is new," said Ostman. He proceeded to introduce Liz Carall and John Owens.

"Those of you who were here last year remember these two instructors," Ostman said as they stood to a round of applause. "New this year is Otto Gottburg, from my university, the University of Manitoba. I'll share in a moment what each of their workshops will cover. I count thirty in our group this year, all returnees, except for the three new students. Minnesota, Wisconsin, Iowa, and Illinois are represented."

Ostman dug in his shirt pocket for a folded sheet of paper, then reached in another pocket for his glasses and put them on. "First, let me say that we are all interested in the importance of education, especially environmental education and at every level from the youngest to the oldest. We are never too young to learn, nor are we too old."

He smoothed the wrinkled piece of paper in front of him on the podium.

"The way I see it," Ostman continued, "after reading many pages of research reports and the writings of international experts, the major challenges we face in the world today are these." He began writing on a big sheet of newsprint attached to a flipchart.

1. Slowing down the effects of climate change
2. Developing sustainable food systems
3. Increasing a shift to clean, renewable energy
4. Protecting the world's supply of clean water
5. Developing a sustaining relationship between the environment and society

Ostman spent a few minutes talking about each point and then summarized, "Of course each of these five points is related to the other four. But topping the list is number one. If the citizens of this globe can expect to survive, we must all learn how to slow down the tremendous changes in climate that we are already experiencing. However, each of these challenges is critical to the future of our planet and each can be addressed through education—indeed *must* be addressed through education if it is to be effective and long reaching. Any questions?"

A hand shot up in the back of the room.

"But people in the Minnesota community where I live never talk about climate change, and the Eagle Party officials punish people who try to speak or write about it."

"You are not alone. I'll bet there's not a person in this room that couldn't say the same thing," said Ostman.

Heads were nodding in agreement.

"That's why you're here at Onthaway Academy: to help gain strategies for teaching taboo subjects like climate change. That leads me to our workshops for this year." He flipped over the newsprint, revealing the schedule:

Each day, except for the last three days:
8–9:30 Liz Carall—Lifelong Environmental Learning
10–11:30 Otto Gottburg—Climate Change
12:00 Lunch
1:30–3:30 John Owens—A Life Undercover
3:30 Free Time
5:30 Supper
7:00 Evening Program
8:30 Campfire
Final Three Days: Discussion of Methods for Nonviolent Protest and
    Persuasion

"In addition, I'll expect each of you to write in your journals every day. We'll do some journal sharing each night around the council ring at the campfire. The campfire is a place where you can think whatever you want to think—about yesterday, about today, about tomorrow. Or you can just sit, watch the flames, and not think at all. Okay! Rest, enjoy the evening. Nothing formal planned. Breakfast at seven."

"Well, what do you think about all this?" Molly asked Patrick as they walked outside to a night filled with stars and the only sound that of a loon calling in the distance.

"I . . . I don't know. All of this is way over my head. I've hardly heard of climate change, and here it's a big deal. And this undercover stuff. It sounds scary. What if we get caught when we're undercover, what then? What happens to people who get caught doing all this stuff?"

"Well," said Molly, "that's why you're here to learn how to do undercover work and not be caught."

Patrick slowly walked toward the campfire that the maintenance man, Hans, had started. Its orange flames cast long shadows into the night. Several other people were sitting around the fire as well, on logs that formed a council ring, as Ostman had referred to it.

Patrick's mind was a muddle. Nothing was clear to him—so many contradictions. He thought he was loyal to the Eagle Party. He was never without his *Guide for a Moral Society*. All the answers he needed to live his life were in this book. That's what his teachers told him anyway. He didn't need to think about much of anything. He also remembered how his father had encouraged him to read books he had saved from the Great Collection— books such as *Swiss Family Robinson* and Henry David Thoreau's *Walden*. His father would ask him questions about these books, especially *Walden*. But that was a long time ago. After his father was hurt at the sawmill, he no longer talked about books. In Patrick's memory, that awful day was like the flame of a candle being blown out. His father essentially gave up trying to help his son see a different world.

And now, sitting by this campfire, he was supposed to think. And he was supposed to write his thoughts in a journal. Journals were forbidden in Crystal River, and now, everyone here had one, and they were being instructed to write in them and share what they wrote. They were told not to take their journals home with them, but leave them at Onthaway, where they would be secure from prying eyes. Beyond the early teachings of his father, Patrick had not been encouraged to think.

He walked away from the campfire, still smelling the smoke that sifted over the Onthaway campus grounds. He walked with his head down, occasionally kicking at a clod of dirt in the trail. Arriving at the bunkhouse and his bunk, he took out his journal and wrote, *I'm supposed to write down my thoughts. Should I do it, when I've been taught that thinking was something I shouldn't do?*

Fourteen

After breakfast the following morning, Patrick found a seat in the meeting area in the back of the dining room. His first workshop would be one led by his Oldster friend Liz Carall. He wondered what environmental learning was all about.

"Good morning everyone," Liz said after everyone had found seats. "I trust you had a good night's sleep and a tasty breakfast." Several heads nodded.

"Most of you were in this workshop last year—but this year we're going to do something a little different. We're going to focus more on how to teach creative and critical thinking skills as a way toward understanding some of the basics for doing environmental education."

Liz asked the attendees to begin by introducing themselves. Most were teachers or had an interest in teaching. The current teachers taught in elementary or secondary schools, and a handful taught at their state's Eagle University. No matter what level, Eagle Party mandates forced each teacher to follow the prescribed curriculum.

"What you are compelled to teach today focuses on workforce development, following rules, being loyal to authority, and not raising questions," Liz said, smiling. "Am I right?" Heads nodded in agreement.

"And you are forbidden to even mention environmental concerns, and of course you do not teach critical and creative thinking?" More nodding of heads.

"Here's an easy approach to developing critical thinking skills. It involves searching for assumptions behind a statement—in other words, what does the statement say without saying it *explicitly*?"

Patrick was listening carefully. He thought, *What is Liz talking about? What in the world are critical and creative thinking?*

Liz continued. "I know this is almost blasphemous, but let's look at *A Guide for a Moral Society*, the book that we're supposed to have with us at all times. Everybody got their book? Anybody need one to refer to? I've got some extra copies." Liz handed out copies to the three people who didn't have one.

She directed the participants to count off by fives, starting with Molly Mason. Then she sent the six groups to seating areas around the room.

"Here's what I want you to do. Arrange your chairs in a circle, select one person to be your recorder-spokesperson, and discuss this question: What are the assumptions behind the guidelines in the book that the Eagle Party requires each of us to have with us at all times? When you have finished with that question, I'd like you to work on a second one: What should be the elements of an ideal society?"

Patrick found himself as the lone student among five teachers, including Molly Mason. He wondered what possible contribution he could make to answering a question he didn't understand. The group selected Molly as their recorder-spokesperson. She looked at him and asked, "Patrick, what do you think are the assumptions behind this book that each of us is required to have?"

Patrick hesitated a bit, ran his fingers through his red hair, and said, "Well, first, what right do we have to question a book that tells us how we should lead our lives?"

A math teacher from Duluth said, "Let me see if I can answer Patrick's question. Patrick, do you believe you have a right, and even a responsibility, to know a lot about something before you accept it?"

"Well, maybe," said Patrick. "But haven't people a lot smarter than me written this book, and don't they believe it is best for our society to follow it?"

The math teacher replied, "But Patrick, just because you think someone is smarter than you, should they be telling you what to do and what not to do?"

"Isn't that how the world works?" asked Patrick, smiling. Several people chuckled.

"Patrick, to put you on the spot a little more," said Molly, "do you think that's the proper way for a society to operate—with a few people telling the rest of us what to do? And by the way, they often are not the smartest people either; they just happen to have money and be in control."

"I guess I haven't thought about it," answered Patrick, shifting his position on his chair.

"Fair enough, but one reason we're here is to learn how to think about things more deeply, especially those that affect our lives and the future of our communities," said Molly.

She turned back to the others. "Back to the assumptions for *A Guide for a Moral Society*. Who has an assumption to share?" she asked, ready to take notes.

"I have one," said the Duluth teacher. "Morals are the most important element in a society."

And like a dam breaking, assumptions began pouring from the group's members.

"We need to be constantly reminded how to act."

"A few people decide how others should live their lives and what's important for their communities."

"The list of rules in the book is complete and sufficient for creating a moral society, assuming that's the most important goal for a society."

"I have all of this down, all good points for discussion," Molly said. "The next step in doing critical thinking is to examine each of these assumptions and discuss their validity."

For fifteen minutes the group did that, reaching a consensus that the assumptions they had listed would stand as stated, providing no one later found evidence to refute one or more of them.

"Okay, now let's spend a few minutes on the second question Liz asked us to discuss: What should be the elements of an ideal society—an alternative to what *A Guide for a Moral Society* suggests. I'll start with a suggestion. Most of you were around before the Eagle Party took power in the US and Congress almost immediately voted to suspend the United States Constitution. I would suggest we take a look at it and see what fits the kind of ideal society for the present time as well as for the future. Our old Constitution included such rights as freedom of speech, freedom of the press, freedom to protest in a group, the right for former slaves and women to vote, and more. These sound like starting places for an ideal society."

Another member of the group offered, "The Eagle Party would like us to forget the 1776 Preamble to the Declaration of Independence: *We hold these truths to be self-evident, that all men are created equal, that they are endowed, by their Creator, with certain unalienable Rights, that among these are Life, Liberty, and the pursuit of Happiness.*" She had obviously committed the preamble to memory.

"All excellent points," said Molly. "So if we were to list some of what we believe should be the elements of an ideal society, what would they be?" She could barely write fast enough as the others offered answers:

> The right for everyone to be treated equally
> An economic system that does not favor one group over another
> Freedom to think and develop one's own conclusions
> Universal respect for the environment
> The right to practice one's religious beliefs, no matter what they might be
> The right to safe food, clean water, shelter, medical care, lifelong education, and personal and family security
> The right for everyone over the age of sixteen to participate in societal decision-making

Liz called the entire group back together for the few minutes left before break time.

"That's good for now," she said. "I'm sure you'll think of more before these two weeks pass. To summarize, what we've just done is some beginning critical thinking, focusing on *A Guide for a Moral Society*. We've first noted assumptions, we discussed the assumptions for validity, then we offered alternative suggestions—the elements of an ideal society. I'm sure you've been wondering when we'd discuss creative thinking. Well, when you began listing elements of an ideal society, you were doing creative thinking." Heads nodded around the room.

"Do you have any questions before we wrap up this first session?" she asked.

"I've . . . I've got to do some critical and creative thinking about we've just done," said Patrick with a big smile on his face. Everyone laughed.

"Just a few words before we break," said Liz. "One of the most important responsibilities as teachers is to help learners develop the skills for critically and creatively thinking about their own lives and how they want to live them, and through collective action determine the kind of community they want to live in. This kind of learning must not only take place in the schools. It must become an attitude, and indeed a passion throughout society. Why? Because the world is changing. Old and new challenges continue to appear. We must move past the idea that as teachers, we are simply preparing people to live in our present society, to work at jobs that now exist. We must teach learners the skills to create a society not yet known, to create jobs that no one now is aware of, and meet environmental challenges that may be more severe than the ones we now face."

Everyone applauded Liz's speech before going on break.

Next, Patrick found himself in the climate change workshop, led by Otto Gottburg. Patrick learned that severe weather, with heavy rains and flooding, was likely to occur more frequently. He learned that because of rising ocean levels, parts of Florida had already been underwater for several years, as well as much of New Jersey, New York City, and several West Coast cities. And just as some areas were underwater, driving people to higher ground, vast areas of the globe suffered from droughts that were destroying crops and creating famines. Huge wildfires in those dry areas destroyed thousands of acres of forestland.

"These devastations will continue, and we can't turn back the clock," Gottburg said. "But the good news is we can slow down the effects of climate change by dumping less carbon dioxide emissions into the atmosphere. We must get the word out. Climate change is a serious threat. And education, helping people become aware of the dire situation we face, can help make what will surely be disastrous less so."

After lunch, Patrick walked down to the lake by himself. He carried his journal with him and he reviewed some of the notes he had taken during the two morning sessions. He had rather enjoyed the first session, the how-to-think session, as he referred to it in his journal. But, although he liked Otto Gottburg's enthusiasm, he had found it more difficult to listen to. This was the first time he had heard about the devastating effect of climate change. He wrote in his journal:

> Can Professor Otto's information be correct? True, we've had some really hot summers, and the rainstorms seem to get a bit worse every year—but I didn't know that parts of the country were flooded when the ocean levels rose. Why didn't we hear about this? This certainly was news. I read the *National Eagle Reporter* news every day. There was no mention of flooding, droughts, and forest fires. Is the Eagle Party not giving us all the news?

Fifteen

That afternoon Patrick listened carefully and often fearfully while John Owens discussed a life undercover. In his opening statement, John said, "The key to working as an Oldster Associate is to have everyone around you believing that you are one of them. Nothing that you say and do should have anyone questioning your loyalty to the group. But, as you know, you are there for two reasons: to inform the Oldsters about what is going on in your group, which for many of you means your school, and to try to make changes—in your case, to change what is taught in your schools and how it is taught."

Patrick listened to these words and remembered something that his mother had told him many years ago: "No matter what you do in life, you must always be honest."

Patrick raised his hand. "But isn't that being dishonest? Ma taught me to always be honest."

"Patrick," John said, looking him in the eye. "What you are expected to do may look dishonest and will likely feel dishonest, but what you are doing is for a greater good. Sometimes we each have to do things that may feel wrong at the time, but in the bigger picture are the right things to do. Does that make sense?"

"I . . . I think so," said Patrick.

John continued. "Let's talk about your first assignment as an informant.

You all realize that the Office for Social Responsibility is reading every email and text message, every kind of communication to make sure that everyone is toeing the mark and is loyal to the Eagle Party and its teachings."

He wrote the words "Acrostic Code" on the flip chart. "This is one of the most popular and useful ways of sending a message to a fellow Oldster Associate or to an appropriate Oldster official. It means that your real message is embedded in another message that hides what you're really trying to say. How many of you are already using this code?" Several hands went up.

"I've asked Molly Mason to explain how she uses the code." Molly walked to the front of the room with a piece of paper.

"Here's what I do," Molly began. "First I decide what I want to communicate—let's say that I feel someone in my school has learned I am working undercover and is prepared to inform the authorities. The message I want to communicate to my Oldster contact person might be 'I am in danger.'" She wrote the words "I AM IN DANGER" vertically on the flip chart.

"Here's a simple example of my message embedded in a false one." She wrote horizontally on the flip chart: "INTERESTING AGRICULTURAL METHODS IN NORWAY. DESTROYING ALL NATIVE GRASSES. ESPECIALLY RYE."

"The first letter of each word forms the message: I AM IN DANGER." She looked around the room. "Any questions or comments?"

She continued. "You can use the second letter, the third letter—it doesn't matter as long as the person receiving the message knows what you are doing. My Oldster contact and I have already established these basic rules. If I'm going to use the first letter of each word to form a message, I write out the month that I use to date the message. If it's July, I write July. If I'm going to use the second letter, I use the number seven to indicate July."

Molly looked around the room. Everyone was listening intently. She continued by asking, "How do we communicate these messages? Using our SPEDs is most efficient. But I also suggest that you send many messages—send several a day, the majority of them *without* secret messages embedded in them. The more decoy messages we send, the less chance the OSR will grab a message and decode it. Send some messages without embedded messages that are as dumb sounding as the one I used as an example. That will help keep them confused."

All of this was completely new territory for Patrick. He had never read about, or even heard about, codes—they obviously were taboo topics for the school curriculum at Crystal River High.

"One more thing," Molly added. "In addition to sending emails to my Oldster contact, I use the old-fashioned way of leaving a note in a secret place that we both agree on. I still code the message in case someone else accidently finds it. I have a secret alert message I send to my contact by SPED when he should look for a message in our secret hiding place. I've been doing all of this for several months, and so far, so good," she concluded.

"Thank you, Molly," John said. "As I said at the beginning, in addition to being an informant, your second responsibility is to help make changes. For all you teachers this means changes in the curriculum and changes in teaching approaches. This is the most difficult, and the most dangerous, part of your assignment. Under Helgi Ostman's direction, we'll spend most of next week studying methods for nonviolent protest and persuasion, with an emphasis on what you can do as an Oldster Associate for the organization. This is something Onthaway Academy has not previously discussed.

"For those of you interested in how to do computer hacking and strategies for computer-generated encryption of messages, stay on. I've arranged for a computer professor from the University of Manitoba to help with this session. His name is Steuart Winter, and he has just arrived."

Patrick's ears perked up when he heard this. He looked forward to learning more about what he thought sounded like more interesting approaches to sending messages than what the group had been discussing.

John Owens tore the sheets of writing from the flip chart, crumpled them up, and dropped them in the huge fireplace at the end of the meeting room. He struck a match to them, and soon the written record of the discussion curled up the chimney in a trickle of gray smoke.

"Have a great afternoon. Oh, and don't forget to take a little time to write in your journals," John said as group members filed out of the big log room, some of them walking to the lake, others making their way back to their bunkhouses.

After an hour's session on computer hacking and encryption strategies, Patrick walked down to the place he had found at noon, next to a big pine tree with a view of the lake. He sat quietly for a time, watching some of the group climb into kayaks and others into canoes. And when they had paddled off, he sat alone, listening to the soft summer breeze move through the white pine needles. He listened to the sound of the lake caressing the stones that lined the shore.

His mind was a tangle of conflicting thoughts. He began writing in his journal:

> I grew up being loyal to the Eagle Party: at one time I dreamed that I might become an official in the party's organization. I am looking forward to becoming a high school teacher, but I have three years of training ahead of me at Eagle University before I can do that. Now, I am expected to do something different. I am supposed to become an Oldster Associate, working undercover for the Oldsters. They seem interested in tearing down the Eagle Party and replacing it with something quite different. Some of what they are suggesting sounds good, but it also sounds like everyone would have to help run the country. Now, most people in the US are quite content to let someone else run the country, as long as they are safe and have food and shelter. Sure, it would be nice if my family could afford health care and have police protection. But the Eagle Party teaches that if you work hard, follow the rules, and not do anything in opposition to the party, your life will be good. At least I know how things work now. Are the Oldsters correct in trying to disrupt this?

Patrick's first week at Onthaway Academy passed quickly. On Friday evening, when the group once again gathered at the council ring before a blazing campfire slicing into the dark night, people readily shared their journal entries. Patrick sat quietly, listening but not sharing. Once again, as he walked back to the men's bunkhouse, he thought about all that he was learning. One important thing he was learning was how to think critically, which made it all the more difficult for him to accept the assumptions behind Onthaway's workshops and its other activities. He didn't confide this to anyone, but he continued to question the basic assumption of the Onthaway Academy, which seemed to be that the American citizens had the right—even the responsibility—to vote out the Eagle Party. And the way to make this happen was through education both in and out of the schools. He didn't know if he wanted to be a part of that. What he did know was that he had gained several new friends, especially Judy and George. And he was getting to know his former teacher, Molly—what a great person she was—and others, too, particularly several of the teachers who had just finished their first year teaching, and had attended one of the Eagle Universities. During their free time, he learned a lot about what to expect at the university—and even got some hints as to how he might work as an Oldster Associate student while working on his degree.

One thing he knew for sure, he would never turn in any of these people to an Office for Social Responsibility—that he would not do.

As he entered the bunkhouse, he saw a bank of clouds building in the west. Crawling into bed, he thought about the fierce thunderstorm he had experienced while at Camp Forward. He thought, *At least I have a roof over my head tonight.* Soon he was fast asleep.

A flash of lightning followed quickly by an ear-splitting clap of thunder awakened him, as it did several others in the bunkhouse. Patrick went to a window and saw a deluge of rain falling so hard he could barely make out the dining hall. Another flash of lightning, another clap of thunder, and then a tremendous "Ka-boomb" shook the bunkhouse. Patrick glanced toward the dining hall and saw flames leaping from the back of the building. He was sure lightning had struck the building, which was soon entirely engulfed in flames. Patrick saw several people running toward the flaming building, some darting inside and carrying out books and chairs and tables. He quickly pulled on his clothes and joined the others lined up from the lake to the burning building, passing pails of water from one to another and tossing the water on the flames. Each pail of water caused a little cloud of steam.

Soon Director Ostman shouted, "It's no use." And everyone stopped carrying water and watched the flames consume the main building of Onthaway Academy—all but one person, who was hiding in the shadows with a special SPED device on which he wrote the following: *Dining and meeting place destroyed. The Onthaway Academy is no more. Agent B.*

Sixteen

When Liz returned to her Crystal River farm, she couldn't rid her mind of the disaster she had witnessed at Onthaway Academy just a few days earlier. She sent a one-word, coded message to Andy. "Home," it read.

It was early evening, and Liz was tired from the long trip back but she needed to talk with someone to share her frustrations and concerns. And she also realized how much she missed Andy.

A half hour later, Andy arrived, as Liz knew he would. They sat together on the back porch of Liz's old farmhouse, where the overhang protected them from the possibility of a drone taking a photo or recording their conversation.

"Glad you're home," Andy said. "I missed you." He looked into Liz's troubled face.

"Missed you, too, Andy, more than you will ever know."

"So how'd the workshop go? How are things at Onthaway Academy?"

"There's no more Onthaway," said Liz. "Lightning struck the main building and it burned to the ground. According to Helgi Ostman, Canada is not likely to rebuild. Andy, this is another cold-as-thunder event. Onthaway was a place that gave us hope. And now it's gone, burned to the ground." Her eyes filled with tears.

"That's awful," Andy said as he put an arm around Liz and pulled her close. "Just awful." They both said nothing for a time.

"Onthaway was the cornerstone of what we Oldsters were trying to do," Liz said quietly. Andy brushed the tears from her face with his handkerchief.

"We were just about to start several days of discussions on how to carry out nonviolent protests and persuasion tactics when it happened. Everything gone. Just like that, with a lightning strike—if it was a lightning strike," said Liz. "Andy, I'm worried that the Social Responsibility people had an undercover agent at Onthaway Academy. It seems a little too convenient for the main building to be struck by lightning just when we were about to discuss some action strategies—some practical ways of starting a social revolution."

"It does at that," Andy said angrily. "But I guess we should expect the Party to play the same game we're playing—trying to find out what the other side is doing."

"It sure looks that way," said Liz.

"Had to be some positive things happen while you were there, though."

"Sure. Molly Mason was there. She's a great teacher. She could become a leader in our social revolution. But she can't do it alone. She'll need all the help we can give her. And frankly, I don't know how to do it. I'm increasingly suspicious that the OSR is becoming aware of what we're trying to do—so we've got to be more careful than ever."

"What about young Patrick O'Malley—how'd he work out?"

"He got through the selection process at Camp Forward with flying colors. He participated in all the Onthaway workshops—but I'm a little worried about him. He was often off by himself, writing in his journal," said Liz. "He seems to be doing a lot of thinking. He keeps reminding us that the Eagle Party is paying his way to attend Eagle University's three-year teacher preparation program. So he's a bit torn about becoming an Oldster Associate for us."

"Probably understandable. Remember, he's grown up with the present system. He doesn't remember what it was like before the Eagle Party took over."

They both sat quietly for a few minutes, holding hands as the sun dipped beneath the horizon, sending rays of red across the darkening sky. Crickets began chirping as the cool night air swept across the big field across the country road from Liz's old farmhouse.

"Andy, there's so much the Oldsters can do, must do, but how can we do it when we are being watched every minute of the day?" asked Liz.

"Have you ever found a Social Responsibility bug in this house, Liz?"

"Nope, never have."

"Then I have an idea," said Andy as he took her hand and led her inside the house and up the stairs to her bedroom.

"If the OSR ever knew," said Liz as she turned back the spread on her bed.

Seventeen

Upon returning home from Onthaway Academy, Patrick O'Malley reported to Crystal River Woodworks for his summer job. The management at the factory, aware that Patrick had been selected to attend Eagle University, didn't hesitate giving him a job. Indeed they couldn't say no, as Patrick had achieved a high-level status in the Crystal River community, with his name officially listed as an Eagle Community Hero, an honor few young people in the community achieved. Most of the names inscribed on the Eagle Heroes Honors Board erected on the lawn outside the Crystal River Social Responsibility Headquarters were managers and top-level executives in the town's various business enterprises in the community.

Except for a handful of Oldster members, no one in the community knew that Patrick had attended Onthaway Academy and was trained to become an Oldster Associate. He didn't even tell his parents, who still believed he had been on a canoe-camping trip to the Boundary Waters. One important thing Patrick had learned from his workshops at Onthaway Academy was to trust no one, and thus tell only those who needed to know that he was trained as an Oldster Associate.

Because of his hero status, Patrick earned ten Eagle credits an hour at his woodworks job, more than the most experienced men working on the production floor. His title was special assistant to the plant manager. He had his own office, which was air-conditioned and away from the noise, dust, dirt, and dangerous working conditions found in many parts of the factory.

After a few days of working in the office, doing filing work, fetching coffee for the plant supervisors, and other such mundane tasks, he became bored and began thinking about Onthaway Academy. He wondered if he might try some of what he had learned there, following the advice he had gotten to be extremely careful about what he did and how he did it, as the consequences could result in everything from a "doesn't always obey rules" note in his employment file (which was permanent and would follow him throughout his employment career, wherever that was and whatever he did), to being jailed, placed in an internment camp, or, for the most flagrant violations, "eliminated." Patrick had heard elimination mentioned only once among the men at the woodworks, when they said a coworker had been eliminated and never heard from again.

Patrick had an idea. He knocked on the plant manager's door.

"Enter," a gruff voice said. Patrick opened the door and stepped inside. He had never been in this office before, and he was immediately struck by how fancy it was: carpeting on the floor, paintings of outdoor scenes on the wall, and a huge wooden desk that had a view to the west, away from the factory.

"Yeah, whatta you want?" said the manager, one of the most unfriendly fellows Patrick had ever met.

"I was thinking," began Patrick.

"That all you got to do, think?" said the manager. He had something in his mouth and was sucking on it. Patrick decided it was a lollipop and almost smiled when he figured out what it was.

"I . . . I was wondering," stammered Patrick.

"You were wondering what?"

"I was wondering if during the noon lunch break I might meet with several of the young guys working on the production floor," Patrick said.

"What the hell for? Them guys needta eat and then get back to work. They ain't got no time to meet."

"I was thinking of asking a half dozen of them if they would like to discuss some of the writings in *A Guide for a Moral Society*, to see if they really appreciate that great book and all of its teachings."

"Well, why in hell didn't you say that in the first place? Sounds like a good idea. Some of them young guys can hardly read, do 'em good to dig into that book a little deeper. My guess is they don't hardly read it at all," the big, lollipop-sucking manager said. "Tell you what, I'll pick out six young guys for you and tell them they gotta report to the conference room tomorrow noon. How would that be?"

"That would be great," said Patrick, who turned and quickly left the office, now wondering exactly what he would do and how he would do it. He thought about contacting Liz Carall for some advice, but then thought better of it. He knew he hadn't quite mastered the coding system he was supposed to follow when he contacted anyone connected to the Oldsters, and if he muffed the message and the OSR saw it, he would be doomed before he ever got started. So he decided to try what he had learned at Onthaway Academy, without any advice. *I suspect Oldster Associates have to do that all the time*, he thought, rather proud of himself. He was also more than a tad concerned about working undercover for the Oldsters, given the good things the Eagle Party had done for him, including handing him this cushy summer job. But on the other hand, he wanted to try for himself at least one of the methods he had learned earlier in the summer.

The next day, Patrick arrived at the conference room before the selected workers arrived. He looked around for a listening device, another skill he had learned at Onthaway Academy, and found none. He assumed, correctly, that the Social Responsibility reviewers wouldn't be wasting their time listening in on the discussions of important people such as those managing the operations of this huge woodworks factory.

A few minutes later, the six young men who had been ordered to attend Patrick's session were in the room. Patrick knew them all. They had attended Crystal River High School with him and had dropped out when they were fifteen because their parents couldn't afford the tuition costs.

"What are you doing here, Patrick?" Don asked. He had been one of Patrick's friends before he dropped out of school and began working at the woodworks. Patrick noticed that the end of one of Don's fingers was missing.

"You work here? I haven't seen you on the floor," Don said.

"I work in the office," said Patrick quietly. He looked around the room at the worn faces of his former schoolmates, at their thickly calloused hands and the many scars from the cuts and scrapes they had experienced since they began working here.

"Oh," was all that Don could say, probably worried that if he said more Patrick would report him for inappropriate language or some other reason that would get him into trouble with the floor supervisor. The others said nothing, each wondering why they were there, using up the few minutes they had to rest after their quick lunch of a sandwich they had brought from home.

"I told the plant manager that we would discuss some writings from *A Guide for a Moral Society*," Patrick began. "I trust each of you has your copy with you." All nodded yes. Everyone had a little pouch that attached to their belt and held a copy of the important guidebook. "But I want to do something different."

Patrick looked around the room at six puzzled faces. He went on. "I've checked this room and there are no bugs. Nobody is listening in on what we are doing here. What we say in this room will stay in this room. I hope I can trust every one of you to tell no one what we talk about here. If you do I'll be in great trouble."

Now each of them was sitting up straight, all looking at Patrick and wondering what was going to happen next.

"My first question is, what do you like about your job? I'll go around the room and ask each of you to give me one thing you like."

The responses varied:

> I earn a little money.
> I have a roof over my head.
> I work inside, out of the weather.
> My income helps my family.
> We've all got food to eat.
> At least I have a job.

"Thank you," Patrick said. "Now I'd like you to tell what you don't like about your job."

Silence. The workers wondered if they could trust Patrick, or if this whole meeting thing was a ruse to cause trouble for them—to get them fired or worse.

"Okay, I'll start," said Don. "About time somebody asked this question." There were many more responses this time:

It's hard work.
Dangerous—too many injuries.
Work is too hard for kids who are only fifteen.
Bosses are mean and expect more than we can do.
Pay is way too low.
Long hours—work fifty hours a week, sometimes more.
Sunday is our only day off.
We are always being watched.
We always have to do a job just as we are told, even if we have a better idea.
It's against all rules to complain.
There is no chance for promotion, even though we were told there was.

The never-before-spoken complaints came like water gushing from a broken hose. But then the time was up.

"We'll meet again next week," Patrick said as he opened the door. And then a little more loudly so people in the outer office might hear, he added, "Be sure to bring your *Guide for a Moral Society* with you."

He returned to his office, feeling quite good about what he had just begun, but at the same time more than a little concerned that he might be found out. He assumed, correctly, that Oldster members were distraught with what had happened at Onthaway, but now he was feeling that maybe education could change some minds; at least his beginning efforts with a few of his old classmates seemed to provide some hope. But then he thought, *How can I ever move these guys toward thinking about the environment and their relationship to it? They're mostly interested in surviving, thinking about their lives and the lives of their families from day to day. Unless their economic conditions can be improved, they'll be the last people who would worry about the environment and how they should relate to it or try to save it. Or are they?*

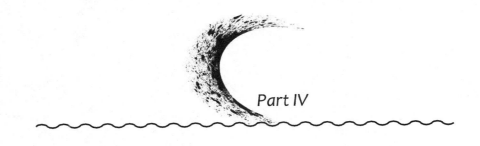

Part IV

July

Eighteen

Joe Stewart, fifty-eight, lean, muscular, with a full head of pepper-and-salt hair, was weary after taking a special jet flight from California to Milwaukee. He was well known within the Washington, DC, Office for Social Responsibility as the "Fixer." He traveled the country, putting out little fires and big ones that had erupted since the Eagle Party took power. He had previously worked for the CIA's counterintelligence unit, where he learned many of the skills he was now well paid for using. Before that he served in the US Army.

"How can I help you?" asked the fortysomething woman who sat in front of an array of computer screens at Wisconsin's Office for Social Responsibility.

"I have an appointment with Mr. Putkey," Stewart said. He glanced at a nameplate that said Mamie Chilson, administrative officer.

Mamie looked at one of the computer screens, which displayed Stewart's photo. "Indeed you do, Mr. Stewart. And welcome to Wisconsin. I note you've never been in our state before."

"That is correct," said Stewart.

"Some coffee?" asked Mamie.

"That would be great, thank you," said travel-weary Stewart.

After one sip of coffee, he was greeted by a tall, gray-haired man wearing a well-tailored suit with a red tie. He entered the reception area from the big door to the left of Mamie's desk.

"Fred Putkey," he said, thrusting out his hand. "But just call me Fred."

"Joe Stewart."

"Heard a lot about you, Joe. Come into my office so we can talk." He extended his arm, allowing Stewart to enter first. Putkey closed the door.

"Here, sit by this table. Do you need a warm-up for that coffee?"

"No, I'm okay." Stewart looked around the office. His eyes fixed on the enormous wooden desk near a window overlooking Lake Michigan. He glimpsed a photo of John Emery, president of the United States, on one corner of the desk. Behind it he saw a matching wooden credenza and a glowing computer screen. In one corner of the office, on separate stands, were the flag of the United States and a huge red Eagle Party flag.

"Heard about the little incident in California," said Putkey.

"Right, a little dicey. Group of Democrats—didn't know there were any left—organized a series of protest marches in Fresno. Their idea was to take over the local OSR. Sure glad nobody had guns. Smartest thing the government did was to suspend the US Constitution and confiscate everybody's guns. You know what? These people had baseball bats. Every dang one of them had a baseball bat."

"I heard that the good guys won."

"It took a little doing, but it got easier when somebody broke the arm of the local OSR clerk with a bat," said Stewart.

"So what really happened? I saw the classified report. Good thing the news wasn't spread across the country, or we'd have more incidents like that."

"Well, the local official ending up with a broken arm was a contradiction of the group's no-violence policy. After that it was easy to learn the name of the group's leader. He's no longer with us—made it look like an accident."

Putkey smiled and said, "Solved the problem."

"And with no leadership, the group evaporated. But we're keeping an eye on the situation. Never can tell when another wild-eyed liberal will step forward. Bunch of fools. Don't know when they have it good."

"Isn't that the truth," said Putkey.

"So why am I here?" asked Stewart. He was a man who didn't like to share details about his successes and the tactics that he used.

"Well," began Putkey. "You've probably heard about these Oldster chapters here in the upper Midwest."

"Yeah, I've heard about them. There was some mention on a Social Responsibility news clip a few weeks ago."

"There are about fifty such groups here in Wisconsin, maybe half that many in Minnesota, a handful in Iowa, and just a few recently organized in northern Illinois. To belong to an Oldster chapter, you have to be at least sixty years old, not working, and willing to volunteer your services to the community and especially to the Eagle Party and its various community activities."

"So what's the problem? Sounds like a bunch of old folks who want to help their communities as well as assist the Party."

"I don't think it's as simple as that. There's this Oldster chapter in Crystal River that's up in central Wisconsin. They're one of the oldest chapters and one of the most active. They meet weekly in a place called the Last Chapter Saloon. We have a listening device in their meeting room, and so far the local OSR has heard nothing but good things."

"So?" said Stewart.

"I have good reason to believe that they're not as squeaky clean as they claim to be. Several times in the past few months, the listening device quit working for an hour or so and then began working again. The local OSR technical guy checked the device, and there was nothing wrong with it. Could have been a power surge, the guy said, but it also could have been disabled during part of their meetings. I have a hunch that the group's been up to no good, and trying to fool everyone that they are a wonderful, upstanding community group intent on supporting the Eagle Party."

"So what do you want me to do?" asked Stewart, taking a sip of the almost-cold coffee, and still wondering why he was in Wisconsin.

"I want you to go up to Crystal River, figure out a way of joining the group, and let me know exactly what's going on and who is calling the shots. If you find out they are for sure not what they claim to be—well I believe you know what to do. I want this thing nipped in the bud. And whatever you do to stop it, I want it to be an example to other Oldster chapters who might have similar ideas."

"But you just said you've got to be sixty years old to belong. You know I'm only fifty-eight," Stewart said, smiling.

"We'll give you a new identity and make you sixty-two. I've gotten an okay from your supervisor in DC, who, like me, wants to keep any uprising from developing."

"Uprising? You believe a bunch of old galoots could cause an uprising?"

"Never can tell what some people will do. There's always somebody who wants things different from what they are."

"That's true," said Stewart. "Surely was the case in Fresno. So what are the details?"

"Your name will be Joe Vogel. Here are your new driver's license and new Eagle credit card." He handed the cards to Stewart, now Vogel, along with a packet and a set of keys. Here's your background story—it's all written here for you to memorize and then destroy. In summary, you are a recently retired engineer who worked for the New Charge Battery Company in Chicago. You moved to Crystal River because of the beauty of the area and a community of citizens with a strong loyalty to the Eagle Party.

"We rented a house for you—right on the Crystal River—pretty place, I'm told."

"I'm not much for pretty," said Stewart. "When there's a problem, I solve it and then move on."

"I understand," said Putkey. "Do not reveal your true identity or your purpose to anyone in Crystal River—I mean anyone. Remember, you are essentially on your own."

They shook hands and Joe Stewart, aka Joe Vogel, got up and left the office.

"Where in the heck is Crystal River?" he asked Mamie Chilson on his way out.

"You'll find it," she said, smiling. "Nice meeting you."

In the parking lot, Joe climbed into the special battery-powered automobile assigned to him. It looked like an ordinary car, but Joe knew at a glance it was outfitted with dark, bulletproof glass, solar panels on the roof to charge its battery, and a frame of special construction to resist any explosive devices that might be embedded in a roadway.

Why do I need a car like this when all I'm supposed to do is join a group of old retired people? What possible danger could they be to me? Joe thought as he drove north on Highway 41. As he stopped at each of the tollbooths, he paid with his new credit card. He was careful to shield the prepaid card each government employee carried to make sure he protected his new identity.

Two and a half hours later, he saw the sign: Crystal River, Population 2,154. As he drove through town, the beauty of the place immediately impressed him. He saw flowers everywhere: hanging baskets of petunias, flower boxes of daylilies and daises and other annuals in front of each business place. He drove by a three-story brick building with lettering that read Office for Social Responsibility. He wondered if the officials here knew he was coming to town. They likely did not, as the State OSR trusted few people with this kind of information. He was clearly on his own. Fred Putkey had made that clear. His only contact would be a message he was required to send directly to Putkey each week.

He saw flowers lining the walkway to the OSR building. Nearby stood an American flag, and next to it the flag of the Eagle Party, twice as large, both fluttering in the summer breeze. He drove past the Last Chapter Saloon, recalling from his briefing that the Oldsters met there. He drove past a little kiosk with a sign that read Tourist Information and Eagle Party Products. Just off the end of Main Street he saw Crystal River High School and more flowerbeds and flags.

He turned off Main Street and arrived at a neat, white house, 128 River Drive—his home for the next several months. It was a tidy, one-story house located directly on the river. It had a single-car garage. His instructions said he would find the house key under a fake rock on the left side of the step by the front door. Finding the key, Joe opened the door and stepped into a neat little living room with a fieldstone fireplace at one end of the room and the door to the kitchen and dining area on the other. A huge picture window looked out over the river. He saw a few rusty tin cans in the river, and some other clutter he couldn't identify. In the kitchen, Joe opened the refrigerator. It was running, but it was empty. There was no food in the cupboards either. Joe scratched his head; he couldn't remember when he had last gone grocery shopping. Then it occurred to him: this was the first time since he was kid that he lived in a real house. Over the years he had lived in safe houses all around the world—in China, Iraq, Russia, France, wherever he had been sent to carry out a mission—and in hotel rooms, so many hotel rooms, the best of the best, and the worst of the worst. And he was always on the alert, sleeping with his nine millimeter Beretta under his pillow and never sleeping soundly. Every strange noise awakened him, scaring him that his cover had been blown. Was a killer close by to do him in? To do to him what he was usually assigned to do to someone else?

I really wonder why I'm here, thought Joe. *What possible harm can come from a bunch of elderly people who want to meet once a week in the back room of a saloon? I'll bet all they want to do is sit around and talk about the good old days and play bingo.*

Joe unloaded the car, leaving his sniper rifle and his Beretta in their cases tucked away in a secret compartment in the car's trunk. He brought his things into the house, putting them in the closet in the little bedroom that also had a window looking out over the river. In this business he had learned to travel light.

A door off the kitchen led directly to a deck, with a picnic table, an old weathered rocking chair, and a small Weber grill—the old-fashioned kind that required briquettes, lighter fluid, and a match. The deck looked down on the Crystal River. Joe settled into the rocking chair. At no time in his long career had he ever been in a place like this. There was no roar of traffic, although he did detect a faint smell of manure in the air. The smell took Joe back fifty years, back to when he was a kid growing up on a Nebraska farm, where the Stewart family raised pigs, sometimes as many as a hundred of them. He knew the smell of hog manure. He remembered all the hard work and his father's demanding ways. *I could never do anything right,* Joe remembered. *Pa was always on me, telling me I didn't even know how to carry a pail of pig slop the right way. God, I hated that old bastard. The day I graduated from high school and enlisted in the army was the best day of my life. Never went back. When Ma wrote that Pa had died, no way I was going back for the funeral. I didn't want that mean old son of a bitch to get any notice from me, even when he was dead. I heard that Ma died a year later. I didn't go to her funeral either.*

Joe realized that he hadn't thought about his growing up years for a long time. *It's surprising how one little smell, to most people an unpleasant one, will bring back so many memories,* he thought. *And not good ones either.*

It had been a long time since Joe had been able to sit without the fear that he might be in danger or the pressure that he should carry out his assignment so he could go on to the next one and the one after that.

He couldn't remember the last time he had sat quietly, by himself, thinking and relaxing. He listened as the rapidly moving water gurgled over the rocks and trash in the river.

He continued to puzzle why the Office for Social Responsibility had sent him here. *Maybe it's because I'm fifty-eight years old, and they think I've lost my edge. They are right about having an edge. I couldn't do my work without it. But maybe I'm not as sharp anymore. Maybe those who look at what I do see something that I don't see.*

He wondered for a moment what he had really accomplished in his life.

Not much. I've traveled the world; did what I was told to do, always had something to eat, a place to sleep—usually. I'm good with a sniper rifle, better than most. But I've never married, never had children, never owned a house. Someone else has always decided for me what I wanted—first the US Army, then the CIA, and now the OSR. What have I missed?

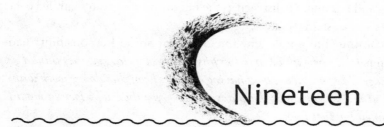

Nineteen

Joe climbed into his car, backed down the driveway, and headed for Crystal River's Main Street in search of a grocery store. He hadn't been inside a grocery store in twenty years so was rather looking forward to it. On the far end of Main Street, he spotted what looked like a mini-shopping mall. In the middle of the small cluster of shops was a big General Grocery store. He had seen the sign several times on his drive up from Milwaukee—he surmised the grocery chain must be big in Wisconsin. He pulled into the parking lot and entered the store. It didn't look at all like the grocery stores he remembered. He saw no one in the store, no checkout lanes, no cash registers.

Joe was puzzled as to what to do. He remembered that last time he was in a grocery store he pushed a cart along an aisle, picked out items he wanted, and then took them to a checkout where they were scanned and he paid. But he saw no checkout lanes, no cash registers, just floor-to-ceiling shelves as far as the eye could see. They were stocked with canned goods, paper products, everything he remembered seeing in a grocery store—but much more of it. It did not look like a grocery store but was more like a warehouse.

"You must be new to General Grocery," said a young woman who appeared from behind what looked like a stack of some kind of cereal. "You order your groceries from your SPED, and they're delivered right to your home within an hour."

Now Joe knew why there were no cars in the small parking lot. "This store is really a storage and distribution center," the young woman continued. "But you can place your order here if you want. You'll still have to wait a half hour for the items to be collected. It's easier if you just do it from home. Just look for the General Grocery app on your SPED, and everything you'd ever want will appear. Just click on the picture. And if you don't know how to prepare something, just click on the item a second time and a recipe will appear. You pay with your Eagle credit card, of course, just like when you order other stuff from your SPED."

"Thank you," Joe said, a bit befuddled. *The world has changed while I wasn't paying attention*, he thought.

Rather than go home and order groceries, he thought he would find a place to eat and maybe a cold beer as well. As he traveled back down Main Street, he decided to stop at the kiosk he saw earlier, the one with the sign Tourist Information and Eagle Party Products. He parked next to a well-tended flowerbed and walked up to the little window.

"How can I help you," said Emily Taylor, smiling broadly. She was wearing a rather revealing sundress. Emily was not afraid to show off her physical attributes. So far the OSR hadn't commented on her manner of dressing. "I haven't seen you before. You must be visiting."

"Yes and no. I am new to town and I'll be living here. I have a house over on the river," said Joe.

"Well, welcome to Crystal River," Emily said, extending her hand. Joe took it. Emily's hand was soft and smooth. She looked him right in the eye. Most people didn't do that with Joe, especially those who knew who he really was and what he was trained to do. She had blue eyes. Sparkling blue eyes.

"Is there a place around here where I can get something to eat?" Joe asked.

"There's a big supper club just out of town; that's quite a good place. It's called the Embers. Kind of expensive to eat there, though," Emily said quietly. "Tell you what, I'd recommend the Last Chapter Saloon. Used to be the library. You can get a good meal there, and they've got beer on tap as well. Say, could I interest you in some Eagle Party memorabilia, maybe a cap, or a T-shirt?"

"How about a cap? I could use a good cap," said Joe, fishing for the Eagle card with his new name on it.

"That will be thirty-two Eagle credits," said Emily, scanning the card, while checking the name. "And thank you, Mr. Joe Vogel. It's none of my business, but are you retired?"

"Matter of fact, I am. I was an engineer at the New Charge Battery Company in Chicago. Heard about Crystal River. Heard it was a good place to retire, so here I am." Joe smiled. It had been a long time since he had carried on a conversation with an attractive woman who wasn't somehow related to one of his assignments. He knew he must see Emily again.

Joe drove the short distance to the Last Chapter Saloon. He remembered Mr. Putkey saying that the Crystal River Oldsters met at this saloon. He parked out front. The place still looked like a library. He remembered the one that he sometimes visited when he was a kid, although his father wasn't big on libraries. "Reading's a waste of time," his father had said. "Especially when there's work to be done." *There was always work to be done on the home farm*, thought Joe.

Joe walked up to the bar, slid onto a bar stool, and looked around. A mounted deer head looked down at him from the wall above the bar. Next to it he spotted a mounted fish that looked to be three feet long–a big fish. *Must be one of those musky fish*, Joe thought. When he was a kid he had read about big fish like this, but he had never seen one. His dad was against fishing. "Big waste of time," he had said.

"What'll you have?" asked the big, burly, bartender.

"Got anything good on tap?"

"Try our local Crystal River Amber. Pretty good, considering," said the bartender. "Cheap, too. Most folks around here ain't got much, but they got a lot of troubles. So they drink a lot of Crystal River Amber. I don't tell them that the Social Responsibility folks don't allow no beer to have more than 2 percent alcohol. OSR folks would rather nobody drank anything but water. Some of them claim drinking beer is the first step toward immorality. So that 2 percent stuff is a kind of a compromise. It ain't water, but not far from it."

The man poured a glass of the weak beer and slid it across the bar to Joe. "You're new here. Ain't seen you around."

Joe extended his hand. "Yup, you're right. Just moved here. Name is Joe. Joe Vogel."

"Bill," said the bartender. He extended a big, ham-like hand. He had a finger-numbing handshake.

"Say, wasn't this once a library?"

"Yup, it was. When the Eagle Party took over the country they decided that a bunch of the books in this place just didn't fit their plans for a moral society. So they organized a big book-burning celebration."

"I remember that," said Joe. "Happened all across the country."

"I can't say the OSR was wrong," said Bill. "People were reading all these books and getting wrongheaded ideas about how to live their lives. Lots of sex stuff in some of those books, too. A moral society's gotta keep a lid on that sex stuff. Perverts out there. People going at it with each other and not being married. Social Responsibility folks had it right."

Wanting to change the subject, but careful not to reveal too much about himself, Joe said, "I heard that a bunch of old-timers meet here every week, is that so?"

"Yeah, that's right. Bunch of retired people. Oldsters, they call themselves. They eat lunch here every Wednesday. Sometimes they sing. Sometimes they play cards. Sometimes they just talk. Don't know what they talk about. I don't care," said Bill. "One thing to their credit, them Oldsters keep this town filled with flowers. I don't think no town around here has as many flowers as Crystal River. Oldsters do that for us."

"Sounds like an interesting group," said Joe. "I saw some of those flowers when I drove into town. Those Oldsters do good work." Joe took a sip of his beer.

"That they do," said Bill.

"Could I have a look at your menu?" asked Joe. "I'm starved."

Twenty

Liz Carall nodded at John Owens. "Taken care of," said John, indicating he had disabled the Social Responsibility bug.

Despite the glorious July weather, nearly the entire membership of the Crystal River Oldsters was in the room. "First, I have some personal news," Liz said, smiling. "Andy, would you come up here?" She beckoned to Andy Schmidt, who was seated a few feet away. Andy was smiling as he walked to the podium where Liz stood.

Liz took his hand. "Andy and I were married last week. Pastor Larry did the honors." After a moment of surprised silence, everyone jumped to their feet and clapped loudly.

"Congratulations," said Emily. "I'm so pleased for both of you."

"Sorry for keeping it so quiet. We didn't want the OSR to know—the less they know about us the better," said Liz. "And now, back to business," she said as Andy returned to his seat still smiling.

"I have some other news, but first, does anyone else have news that we should know about since we last met?" Liz asked.

"I met a fellow yesterday," began Emily. "He stopped by the kiosk. His name is Joe Vogel. Said he just retired and moved here from Chicago. Seemed like a heck of a nice guy, maybe a potential Oldster member."

"Can you follow up?"

"I'll see what I can do," said Emily. "Other than that, Eagle memorabilia sales are going wonderfully well. People keep buying this stuff. Believe me,

I don't know why. But I keep selling it because I know what we earn goes to a good cause."

"Well, my news is much worse," said Liz. "For those of you who may not have heard, Onthaway Academy is no more." Several members were shaking their heads in confusion and shock. Obviously the word had not gotten to everyone. Even with their coded message system, it was difficult to keep everyone informed. Several members, even though they were required to have their SPED communication devices with them at all times, occasionally forgot to turn them on, or to keep them in bright light long enough so their solar batteries would remain charged.

"Lightning struck the main building while we were there, and it burned to the ground. At least that was the official take on what happened. To make things worse, the word is the Canadian government has become squeamish about the whole idea of the academy and its purpose. Apparently they don't want to create any more waves with their neighbor to the south than they already have, so they don't plan to rebuild."

"So what are we going to do?" asked Emily. "Onthaway has been the single most important way to train our Oldster Associates."

"The academy has done an excellent job," Liz agreed. "But the results haven't been that good, I'm sorry to say. Our educational system has changed very little. An Oldster Associate teacher or two in a school just isn't enough to make a difference. Everything that every teacher does is watched by the OSR people. Our Oldster Associates try to do one new thing: they try to bring a group of students together to discuss what they are learning as Molly Mason did this past year, and the school administrators quash the idea before it ever gets going."

"You're right, Liz," said Emily. "As far as I can see, little has changed in the Crystal River schools, nor in any of the other schools in the region. Molly is a good undercover agent in the school, and of course she's going to begin meeting with us as liaison when school starts again this fall. We've also got young Patrick O'Malley; he's headed for Eagle University in the fall and is working a summer job at the woodworks here in town . . ." Emily's voice trailed off.

"I have an idea for us to consider," said Liz. "I don't know if the OSR folks will come after us for this, but I think it's worth a try."

"We've got to try something," said John Owens. "I don't think trying to change education from what we have now is working as a way toward our social revolution. What's your idea, Liz?"

"What if we set up a series of what we call sharing sessions, inviting people in our community to meet and discuss their personal histories? We might have a session on farming in the past, another remembering the Fourth of July celebration, and certainly one on what people remember about their schooling."

"How would we get this past the OSR?" asked John. "They are not keen on people meeting, no matter what reason."

"Here's my thought. We'll promote the purpose of these sharing sessions as a way for people to recall how things were in the past, with the idea that they will be more pleased with the ways things are now when they make the comparison," Liz said.

"You sure that argument's going to fly with OSR?" asked Emily.

"Well, we won't know unless we try. And besides, what I pick up is the OSR people are getting more complaints every day from the cost of health care, which most people can't afford, to why their wages remain low, to why the roads are in such poor repair. OSR tries to tamp down these complaints, but they still crop up."

"I suggest we start with old-time farming methods. That shouldn't cause any ripples with the OSR folks," said Liz.

A week later, a sign appeared on the bulletin board at the Last Chapter Saloon:

> **Farming Yesterday**
> Remembering How It Was
> Applauding How Much Better It Is Today
> Meet here, next Sunday, 2:00 p.m.

Liz checked her SPED every day for a message from OSR, but she heard nothing. Likely they planned to listen in on the session with their planted bug, which of course John would not disable.

Six former farmers, all of them now working at Crystal River Woodworks, showed up for the first session.

"Thanks for coming," said Liz as they filed into the saloon. The men sat with their hands on their laps, each with big, calloused fingers from years of hard manual work.

"I represent the Oldsters," Liz began. "We are doing a series of these sessions to help people remember how things once were, and how much better they are today." She said this as clearly as possible, so any OSR officer who might be listening would assume this "sharing session" posed no threat to how people were living their lives today. Liz purposely did not ask for the participants' names because she didn't know what these men would say, and she didn't want to get into trouble.

"Farming was hard work," the first man began. He was slightly bent over and walked with a limp. "We got up at five in the morning and milked cows by hand with a lantern to light our way because we had no electricity. Ten cows I milked. Some of them tried to kick me. All of them swatted me with their dirty tails. A miserable job."

The second farmer chimed in. "Same deal with me. No electricity. Milked cows by hand. Drove a team of horses. Hard work. Seven days a week. Every day of the year. Worked on Sundays, too. Worked every day. Better off today. Get Sundays off, and don't have to be to work until seven. Sure beats being out in a stinky barn by five thirty in the morning. Don't earn much today, but if the wife and I stay healthy, we've got nothing to worry about."

Liz was concerned about the fellow's implication about the current state of affordable health care. But she didn't say anything, as the next former farmer almost immediately chimed in. He was an older fellow with gray hair, and twisted fingers, no doubt from arthritis.

"What I wanna talk about is thrashin'. I tell ya trashin', when we went from farm to farm followin' that big old thrashin' machine and workin' our tails off—I was just a kid then. It was something! A special time every summer."

"How so," asked Liz, who was too young to have experienced threshing on her home farm.

"Two things about it was special. All the neighbors got together, telling stories, playing tricks on each other, that sort of thing. The other was the meals. I tell you we had the best meals. Those farm women all tried to outdo each other with their cookin'. I mean we had meat and potatoes, of course, but we had pies of every kind, apple pie, cherry pie, and cakes, chocolate cake, spice cake. Well, just about anything you'd ever want in the way of good things to eat." He paused for a minute and looked down at his hands. He had tears in his eyes. "I miss those days. I really do. 'Course now I'm too damn old to work that hard, or eat that much. Happy with the job I got at Crystal River Woodworks. Bunch of good guys there." He smiled as he gestured at the other men in the room.

A week later, Liz set up a second meeting with a focus on schooling. This time only four people showed up for the sharing session: Aaron and Barbara O'Malley and another couple who had children in school. Everyone knew that the OSR didn't want people gathering, no matter what the stated purpose. And nobody wanted to be on the Social Responsibility's black list. At worst you'd lose your job, and at best you'd probably have your hourly pay rate dropped.

"What do you remember about going to high school?" Liz asked to get started.

"That's a long time ago," said Aaron. "Don't remember much. Must say, though, that we're mighty proud of our son, Patrick, who just graduated from Crystal River High School and got himself a scholarship to go to the big Eagle University up in Marshfield. Kid's planning on being a teacher. Imagine that. I dropped out of high school because my folks couldn't afford keeping me in school, and Patrick is headed for college, with all his expenses paid, too."

When Liz looked at the other couple, the fellow spoke up. "High school was okay." He was short, with a well-trimmed black beard. "Wouldn't have the job I got now without my high school learning."

"What about Crystal River High School today?" Liz asked.

"Don't know much about it. Our kids are still in grade school. Kind of expensive. Expect I'll encourage my kids to drop out as soon as they can — dropout age is fifteen, I believe," the fellow said.

Those few comments were all that she heard that entire afternoon. Both couples seemed afraid to talk, with many of the same fears the former farmers had. The O'Malleys did seem genuinely pleased that their son had won a scholarship to attend the three-year teacher preparation program at Eagle University, however. Liz surely couldn't blame them for that.

Liz and the two couples talked for a bit about the weather and how beautiful the flowers in town were this year. But there was no further mention of schooling, even when Liz at one time asked, "Anything else you'd like to say about the schooling in Crystal River?"

She got not a single word from the O'Malleys in response, and a curt "Nope" from the fellow with the black beard.

Liz couldn't believe that so few people were willing to attend what she thought would be interesting sessions. She hoped the meetings would be an entry for people to begin looking at the lives they were now living, and recognizing that they could do so much better. She had taught a similar process when she worked for Badger State University, using an approach called "consciousness raising." But the folks who attended these sessions were likely too afraid of losing the little they had to risk becoming aware of something that might be better. She even had John disable the listening device in the room for the second session, hoping they might have an in-depth discussion of the poor quality, highly slanted education the community's young people now received, and what they could do to help the Oldsters to make it better. But it was not to be.

After the sessions, she thought, *If I can't get people to talk about their present situation, how can we ever move them to talking about the environment and how people should relate to it, and how important it is for them to start now to slow down the environmental destruction taking place. Don't these people care? Or are they so concerned about living their lives day to day that they aren't even aware of these environmental challenges that one day will affect everyone?*

Twenty-One

Three days after Joe found his way to Crystal River, he sent Fred Putkey the following message:

> Arrived in Crystal River safely. Settled in. Looked over the town. Met one Oldster. Will work on becoming a member. Stewart.

Joe had been thinking a lot about Emily Taylor. He didn't know what it was, but it was a feeling different than he had ever had. He felt he must get to know her better. He didn't know if she was married or divorced or a widow; all he knew was she was a member of the Oldsters and she was one of the most beautiful women he had ever met. During his long career, he had met many women. And he had long known that women could be trouble—at least his superiors had warned him of that many times. "Use them, but don't let them use you," one of his training officers had said.

He suspected that if he made a good impression on Emily, she could be his way into the Oldsters, but for the first time that he could remember, he had feelings that he couldn't understand. For Joe, using one's head to analyze and plan was critically important for any mission he was called to do. But he always tried to keep any feelings he might have had in check. Now, his feelings about Emily were at the same time both troubling and interesting.

After sleeping in for a bit on a bright Monday morning and then eating a big breakfast of bacon and eggs, Joe backed his car out of the garage and drove to the little kiosk on Main Street.

"It's Joe?" Emily said when he stepped up to the little window. "Don't tell me your cap didn't fit and you're back for a replacement," she said, smiling.

"Cap fits just fine. And thanks for the recommendation for the Last Chapter Saloon. Interesting place. Good food. Heard that your Oldster group meets there. Also heard some good things about the group, especially about how you're responsible for all these flowers I've seen around town."

"Thanks," said Emily. "It's a lot of work, but our members seem to enjoy doing it. The Eagle credits we earn selling Eagle memorabilia pays for the flowers. Selling Eagle caps and T-shirts and this other stuff is our only income-making activity."

"Any chance you might need some help?" Joe asked.

"You know, I just might. Got word a bit ago that a busload of visitors is coming to town. The buses always stop here. They'll be here in about a half hour."

"What do you want me to do?"

Emily opened the door to the kiosk—there was room for two people, barely, in the place. It been a long time since Joe had been this close to a woman, especially one who got him thinking thoughts that he hadn't had for many years.

Emily showed Joe the shelves of memorabilia, including copies of *A Guide for a Moral Society*.

"We're all supposed to have a copy of the *Guide* with us at all times, but somebody is always losing their copy, or it just plain wears out and they want to replace it. We sell a lot of them."

"What's your story, Emily? How'd you find yourself in Crystal River and a member of the Oldsters?" Joe asked as they waited for the busload of customers to arrive.

"It's a short story. I was born and raised right here in Crystal River. I graduated from Crystal River High School and then went on to Badger State University, where I got a teaching degree. I was an English teacher right here. Didn't get far from home at all."

Joe was a bit hesitant to ask, but he did. "Husband, kids?"

"No husband, no kids. Never married. And what about you, Joe? I remember you said you were an engineer and worked for a company in Chicago. Family?"

"No family. No wife, no kids. Company had me traveling around a lot. Never had time to settle down," Joe said quietly. "Born on a farm in Nebraska. My old man was mean to the core. Could never do anything right for him. I couldn't wait to graduate from high school and leave home. Went off to the U of Nebraska and got a degree in engineering." He was surprised to find himself mixing part of his own true story with Joe Vogel's backstory.

The big tour bus stopped in front of the kiosk and well-dressed people began lining up in front of the little window. Joe searched the shelves and found the items that people wanted, while Emily took care of running the charges through the charge machine. They did a brisk business, and then everyone lined up, climbed back on the bus, and was gone.

"Whew," said Emily, wiping her brow with her hand. "Sure glad you were here to help; I don't know what I would have done with that many people."

"Glad to help," said Joe. "It was a pleasure." Then Joe took a big risk. "Would you be interested in going out to dinner with me tonight, at this Embers place you mentioned the other day?"

"Sure," said Emily, smiling. "I close up the kiosk at five, and then I usually head home. Tell you what—I'll be ready about six. That sound okay?" She wrote her home address on a piece of paper along with the number to use to reach her on her SPED.

"Sounds good to me," said Joe. "See you at six."

When Joe returned to his bungalow on the river, he took out his SPED, which was equipped to automatically encrypt messages. He wrote:

Attention: Director Putkey

Have made good contact with an Oldster member. Have impressed this member. I believe she will recommend me. More later. Stewart.

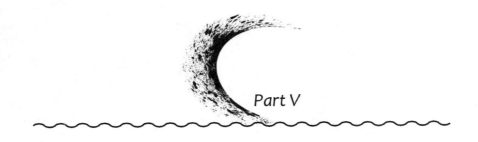

Part V

August

Twenty-Two

Liz Carall called the August meeting of the Oldsters to order. She pointed to John Owens to make sure he had remembered to disable the listening device in the room. He nodded in the affirmative.

"Well, good to see you all again," Liz began. "I hate to begin this way, but it's been a tough summer for the Oldster organization. We lost Onthaway Academy, my effort to get community people to tell their stories fizzled, and we are not making much progress with our hopes for a social revolution. There are two pieces of news, however. Emily, share yours first."

"Thank you, Liz," began Emily. "Remember me mentioning a possible new member at the last meeting? Well, several of us did some background checking and found absolutely nothing. But as you all know, it's impossible these days to do much digging without stirring up OSR concerns about what we are doing. Anyway, with the information we have, we decided that Joe Vogel would be a good fit for our group. I've discussed this with Liz, and she agrees. Let me review a little of Joe Vogel's background before I ask you to vote."

Emily shared some of Vogel's personal history: that he was a retired engineer who had been working in Chicago, that he grew up on a Nebraska farm, and that he chose Crystal River as a place to retire because he had heard it was a pretty place with many good people.

"And," Emily continued, "for the past several weeks he's been volunteering with me at the kiosk. He's a friendly guy, knows how to work, and

I believe he would be an excellent addition to our group." She did not mention that she had fallen head over heels for the guy and that they had been sleeping together. "Of course," said Emily, "I've said nothing to Joe about our real purpose. He is convinced we volunteer our services to make our community more beautiful."

"Are we ready to vote on Joe Vogel's membership in the Oldsters?" Liz asked.

"If Emily and you think he is okay, then I vote yes," said John.

"Okay, everyone in favor of asking Joe Vogel to join our group, hold up your hand."

Every hand went up.

"Wonderful. Assuming you all would agree with my recommendation, I brought Joe along," Emily said. "He's waiting in the bar. So if someone would ask him to come in, we'll introduce him to the group."

Soon a smiling Joe Vogel was standing beside Liz and Emily as the members clapped, shook his hand one by one, and welcomed him to the Crystal River Oldsters.

Liz, with a serious look on her face, turned to Joe Vogel and said, "Now that you are a member of the Oldsters, you are bound to secrecy concerning what we discuss at these meetings. Do you agree to do so?"

Feigning surprise at Liz's request, Joe said, "Yes, yes of course." *What do you know?* he thought. *The Social Responsibility folks were right. This group has a purpose beyond what they want you to believe.* In the weeks that he had been spending time with Emily, he had detected nothing suspicious in her behavior—though, granted, he had been distracted by her sparkling eyes and other charms. Not once had she even hinted to Joe what the Oldster group really had topmost on its agenda.

"So that you know right up front, none of this exists in writing and nothing I say can leave this room." Liz paused for a minute and then continued. "We Oldsters are committed to returning this country to its democratic roots. We are very concerned about what has been happening to the environment in recent years, especially the lack of attention to climate change and its effects. Several of us Oldsters are retired educators. We firmly believe progressive lifelong education that includes not only educational basics such as literacy, history, geography, and the arts but also an emphasis on critical and creative thinking is essential for everyone, from preschoolers to senior citizens. We believe that once we have a citizenry that experiences this kind of progressive lifelong education, we will no longer have a two-class society where the rich have everything and the rest have essentially nothing. We believe education, health care, police, fire protection, and roads are the responsibility of the government, paid for with taxes, and should not be for-profit enterprises. We especially believe the government should take the lead in helping us protect our water and our air from pollution, and our land from erosion. I could go on, but this is the essence of what we believe and the goals toward which we are working."

Joe listened carefully, trying not to show his surprise at the deeply held beliefs of the group and its ideas for essentially overthrowing the present Eagle Party by means of educational reform.

"I must say, I'm most impressed with what your group is trying to accomplish. Most impressed," Joe said. *These Oldsters are a committed group,* he thought. *I can see now why the OSR wanted me here.*

"Now let's move on with our meeting," said Liz. "I've asked Molly Mason and Patrick O'Malley to join us." She turned back to Joe to explain. "Molly is an English teacher at Crystal River High and is our new liaison person with the high school. Patrick is a former student of hers who has a scholarship to attend Eagle University this fall. He is working at the woodworks this summer. Molly is one of our Oldster Associates and Patrick attended Onthaway Academy and is training to be an Oldster Associate. Ask me after the meeting and I can tell you about Onthaway."

Joe was astounded to hear how organized the Oldsters were, and that they had trained what amounted to undercover agents. He was thinking how ironic it was that he, too, was an undercover agent, one with quite different marching orders from his superiors.

There was a knock on the door. "Come in," said Liz, and both Molly and Patrick came into the room.

"I'm not sure that all of you have met Molly, but I'm sure you remember hearing about her and her special role at Crystal River High. Molly recommended Patrick as a candidate for Onthaway Academy, which he attended a few weeks ago."

"It's great to be here," said Molly. "I'm looking forward to attending more regularly once school starts this fall. I want to introduce you to Patrick O'Malley, quite an outstanding young man, who, as some of you know, was recently declared a Community Hero by our local Office for Social Responsibility. Of course they have no inkling that he is also training to be one of our Oldster Associates. Patrick has an interesting story to tell."

Patrick stood up, ran a hand through his red hair, and began.

"First," he said, "I want to thank you for paying for my canoe trip." He grinned because he knew everyone in the room had known it was far more than a canoe trip. "Miss Mason knows that I've been struggling with the idea of becoming an Oldster Associate. It's kind of a slap in the face to the Eagle Party that is paying my tuition to attend Eagle University, which I will do come fall. But I've been thinking about my folks, and the very difficult time they've had, and all the sacrifices they made so I could finish high school. I've never forgotten how my dad almost lost his job at the woodworks when a saw cut off his finger and we couldn't afford health insurance or a doctor. My grandfather burned the stub of his finger to stop the bleeding. I can't forget the awful sound of my dad screaming and the smell of burnt flesh. And then how my mother worried that my dad might lose his job because he had trouble meeting his daily quota.

"So the more I thought about what I learned at Onthaway, the more I began believing in what this group is trying to do and the importance of it so that more people, not just the rich, can lead a decent life. And I've also come to believe that yes, we must pay attention to the environment, and try to correct the problems that have emerged in the past several years before it's too late."

Patrick took a drink of water and once more ran his fingers through his hair.

"As Miss Mason mentioned, my summer job is in the office at the woodworks. I mostly do filing, carry around coffee, and, can you believe it, make more per hour than my dad, who has worked there for many years. I thought I might try a little experiment, try one of the ideas I learned at Onthaway."

Patrick took a couple of minutes to explain the process of consciousness raising, which had as its overall purpose helping people become conscious of their present situation, the first step before deciding what changes they might want to make.

"Here's what I tried," Patrick said. "Company management selected six young men, all of whom had attended high school with me and who had dropped out at age fifteen to work at the woodworks plant. We met in the company conference room, which I checked to see if it was bugged. It was not. We spent the time talking about what they liked about their jobs and what they don't like. At another meeting we'll talk about what changes they'd like to see. I know these guys. I knew them when we were in high school together. They've pretty much given up and expect to work in this factory for the rest of their working lives. It's a dangerous place to work, I might add. But after just one meeting, they seem to have some hope. We'll see where it goes. I know I'm taking a big risk. If one of the boys decides to turn me in, all will be lost. But like I learned at Onthaway, being an Oldster Associate means taking risks. Trying to make change means taking a risk."

Patrick sat down as the group applauded his remarks.

Twenty-Three

Everyone in Crystal River knew Bill the bartender at the Last Chapter Saloon. He was always there, a friendly face, greeting people, pouring glasses of beer, taking orders for meals. People liked Bill. They saw him as an ordinary, good guy. But no one in Crystal River knew that Bill was also a secret agent for the Wisconsin Office for Social Responsibility and had been for several years. Not even the local OSR had been told about Bill.

Bill knew just about everyone in Crystal River, which made him an excellent agent. He knew personally all the Oldsters, as he saw them almost every week. He knew that the local OSR had a listening device in their meeting room, but he thought nothing of it because they had listening devices in all public places.

Bill had his own bug, a tiny but extremely sensitive microphone that could pick up sounds through walls. He had installed it behind the big musky that was prominently displayed in the back of the bar. And while most folks had noticed that Bill wore what appeared to be a hearing aid, it was actually a receiver that allowed him to hear everything that went on in the back room of the saloon.

For a long time Bill had thought that the Oldsters were what they said they were: retired people interested in beautifying their community and helping the Eagle Party by selling memorabilia. It was quite by accident that Bill, after listening in on another group in the bar's backroom, had left his listening device on during an Oldsters meeting. He had been astonished to hear what they were attempting to do. Bill had alerted the state Office for Social Responsibility.

Another practice of the OSR was to keep tabs on undercover agents they sent in the field. Bill was keeping tabs on Joe Vogel. He automatically received copies of every communication that Joe sent and received.

After the Oldster meeting ended and Bill jovially said good-bye to the members passing through the bar on their way out, he sent a message by SPED to the Milwaukee office:

Vogel was voted into Oldsters. He heard directly about what their real mission is—creating what they call a social revolution. I'm eager to see what steps he has in mind to put out this little fire, which could become a much larger one if their ideas catch on. Agent B.

It was a couple hours later that Bill received a copy of the encrypted message Joe sent to Fred Putkey at the state OSR:

I've succeeded in becoming a member of the Crystal River Oldsters with a unanimous vote. I am carefully monitoring their activities to see if they are doing anything beyond their stated purpose as you suspect. So far I believe that they are what they claim to be—interested in making Crystal River a better place and helping the Eagle Party. One of my volunteer tasks has been to help sell Eagle memorabilia. I believe you have gotten inaccurate information about the group. I will continue to carefully observe all of their activities, but so far, nothing looking out of line. Stewart.

Bill read Joe's message, and then read it a second time. Stunned, he thought, *Why is he lying about what he learned at the meeting? What's going on with this guy? He has a reputation for being one of the most formidable fixers the Eagle Party has. I'd better keep an eye on him.*

Twenty-Four

Each year the Crystal River Office for Social Responsibility, in an attempt to pacify and keep the citizens in the community content and feeling patriotic, sponsored a weekend Eagle festival in late August. The local OSR required the various businesses in the community to donate ice cream, beer, and bratwurst for the event, which was free to those who attended. Part-time farmers like Liz and Andy Schmidt were encouraged to have a booth where they could sell fresh vegetables. And of course the Oldsters had a huge booth where they sold Eagle memorabilia.

Bill the bartender manned a booth where he gave away Crystal River Amber Beer. But he had another mission. Bill and the state Office of Social Responsibility decided that Joe Stewart could no longer be trusted to take out the Oldster leadership, and indeed was helping them with their plans for some kind of social revolution. The state OSR had given Bill orders to eliminate Joe Stewart aka Joe Vogel, and a week ago they sent him to a one-day training session at Fort McCoy's Eagle Militia Training Center. Bill had trained at Fort McCoy a year earlier on the use of C4 explosives.

As luck would have it, he had the same training officer this time around, a tall and muscular soldier clad in camouflage.

"You've developed quite a reputation for yourself, Bill," the officer, a captain, said as he took his place in front of a screen on the far wall of the training room. "Word on the Eagle Network is that you blew up the main building at Onthaway Academy, with everyone thinking it was a lightning strike. C4 really does the trick, but it's hard to hide an explosion, which you managed to do. Good work."

"Thank you," Bill said. He added that he didn't want praise but was eager to get on with the training and return home. He had told people back in Crystal River that he was going on a fishing trip. He had said the same thing when he blew up the main building at Onthaway Academy. That time he had gotten excellent intelligence from the Homeland Security satellite that identified the Onthaway Academy campus, after Homeland Security had gotten a tip from the border patrol to do some special reconnaissance of the area just north of the Minnesota border.

Now the trainer said, "We, in the extermination unit, believe we can help you do your job without anyone knowing you are doing it. It's too bad that we've still got some unbelievers in this society who can't seem to follow the Eagle Party rules. Sometimes the only answer is extermination."

Bill said that he understood that completely. He didn't reveal that his target was a turned OSR operative. The officer continued. "We have some sharpshooters in our unit, guys left over from the wars this country fought back in the bad old days. But just like with C4, it's damn near impossible to make an assassination with a rifle look like an accident." Bill told the training guy that it had been a while since he had shot a gun.

"Guns are the old-fashioned way of doing things," the officer said. "Poisons are much more effective and much easier to hide. My preferred material is batrachotoxin."

"Never heard of it," said Bill.

"Have you heard of poison dart frogs?"

"No, can't say that I have," Bill said.

"Well, the skin of these little frogs, which are only about the size of the end of your thumb, contain the most powerful naturally occurring neurotoxin known to mankind. It's many times more powerful than cyanide."

The training officer explained how the Amazon Indians coated the ends of their hunting darts with the material from these frogs. The toxin would kill an animal or a bird in an instant. "One dose of this poison—it's equivalent to two grains of table salt—can kill a person. It almost immediately causes paralysis and directly affects the heart muscles. The person appears to have a heart attack and is dead within minutes."

The training officer went on to show Bill how to use the poison. He sent him home with a small vile half-filled with the poison, and a syringe. The last words the training officer told him were, "Take good care of this stuff. It doesn't care who or what it kills." He laughed loudly when he said it.

On the trip back to Crystal River, Bill was thinking, *I've never used poison to eliminate someone. Scares the hell out of me. Shooting someone, I know how to do, and blowing up is something I know how to do. But using poison, hell, what if I accidently poke myself with the needle? Geeze, I'd be a goner before I ever knew what happened.*

The Saturday of the Eagle Festival weekend dawned bright and clear. A rainstorm the night before had eliminated much of the pollution from the air, and a slight breeze was blowing, sending the ever-present stench from the mega hog farm in a different direction.

Liz and Andy had set up their vegetable stand earlier that morning, bringing to town freshly dug red potatoes, carrots, beets, leaf lettuce, several big heads of broccoli, six large early cabbages, a pail of cucumbers that Andy had picked the previous day, a small basket of zucchini, and a container of tomatoes. By noon they were doing a brisk business, as their prices were low and affordable to the working-class people who made up most of the citizenry of Crystal River.

Joe Vogel and Emily Taylor were doing well at the Eagle memorabilia kiosk and were thoroughly enjoying each other's company as usual. Bill set up his portable bar in a small tent near the kiosk, where he was busily handing out free Crystal River Amber. He had tucked away in his pocket, in a special protective case, the syringe half-filled with the deadly frog poison—he could never remember its fancy name. His task seemed simple enough. All he had to do was stick Joe with the needle and in a matter of minutes Joe would be dead. The challenge, of course, was catching Joe by surprise and sticking him with the deadly needle without anyone knowing what he had done.

John Owens had led several people on a tour of the Crystal River gardens, He was surprised at the interest, knowing that most people in Crystal River did not have flower gardens, couldn't afford flower seeds, and were much more concerned with earning enough Eagle credits so they could simply survive. As people toured the gardens, many of them were smiling. A smiling face was not often seen in Crystal River.

Patrick O'Malley, along with several other office members from Crystal River Woodworks, was in charge of grilling bratwurst and chicken. The pleasant smell of the grilling food soon filled the air. People lined up for the free food.

Bill turned his bartender duties over to another volunteer and slowly walked to the kiosk where Joe and Emily were working. Perspiring heavily, Bill tried to calm himself as he walked toward the kiosk. He felt in his pocket to make sure the syringe was in place and ready to go. He had a plan. He would ask Joe to step out of the kiosk and then he would plunge the syringe into his arm, put the syringe back into the protected case in his pocket, and return to his duties at the beer tent. In a few minutes, Joe would be dead, and his mission would be accomplished.

But Bill couldn't get out of his head that Joe had become a good friend—this was before he knew that Joe had turned and was no longer trustworthy as an undercover agent. Even when he knew what Joe was supposed to be doing, he still liked the guy. Joe had stopped by the Last Chapter Saloon many times, just to chat and have a beer. *Wasn't there another way of dealing with Joe without killing him?* thought Bill. *But I've got my orders. I have no other choice.*

"Hi there, Bill," Joe said as the bartender approached the kiosk. "How's business at the beer tent?"

"Pretty good. Free beer is a big draw. Say, Joe, could you step outside for a minute? I have something to tell you."

"Sure," Joe said. "Emily can hold down the fort." He winked at Emily as he stepped toward the door.

Joe stepped outside and met Bill in back of the little building, a place not readily seen by passersby.

"What can I do for you?" Joe asked, and then he added, thrusting out his hand to shake Bill's, "You've been a good friend, one of my first real friends here in Crystal River, outside of Emily. I really appreciate your kindness and your big smile. Not many people are smiling here in Crystal River."

As he spoke, Joe noticed that Bill was sweating profusely and that his hand was wet with perspiration.

"You all right, Bill? You don't look so good."

Bill retrieved the syringe from his pocket and brought it up to a few inches from Joe's arm. "I'm sorry, Joe. These are my orders from OSR. I'm so sorry." He hesitated a moment before attempting to plunge the needle into Joe's arm.

Joe's training instantly kicked in. He stepped aside, grabbed Bill's arm with the hand holding the needle, and spun him around, trying to move Bill's arm behind him. In the process, the needle entered Bill's thigh before it dropped to the ground. Almost immediately, Bill fell down, clutching his chest. Joe carefully picked up the syringe and dropped it in the nearby trash can. He also searched Bill's pockets for Bill's SPED.

Then he yelled, "It's Bill the bartender. He's passed out. We need help here."

While he was waiting for the ambulance to arrive, Joe sent the following message to Putkey at OSR in Milwaukee using Bill's SPED: *Mission accomplished!*

Soon an ambulance was on the scene, and with sirens screaming and lights flashing it roared off toward the medical facility. Later that afternoon, word came that Bill had died of an apparent heart attack.

"Are you okay, Joe?" Emily asked after she heard the news.

"Not really," Joe said. "Bill was a good friend. He was a friend to everyone in Crystal River."

But what had really shaken Joe was the stunning realization that Bill, in addition to being a well-liked bartender, was also a special agent for the OSR. Joe thought, *This really confirms my decision to leave behind my days as a fixer with the OSR. I knew they would probably come after me when they found out I was seeing Emily Taylor and helping the Oldsters. But try to kill me?*

Joe had trouble concentrating on what he was doing the rest of the afternoon. He could sense that Emily was becoming increasingly concerned about him. Now Joe faced a big decision. Should he tell her who he really was and what his background had been, and what really happened outside the kiosk? He was spending most nights with her; how long could he keep being who he wasn't?

Joe was about to turn to Emily when a young man approached the kiosk. "I'd like an Eagle cap," he said. Joe went to the shelf where the caps were lined up, found one, and handed it to the young man, who in turn handed Joe his Eagle credit card.

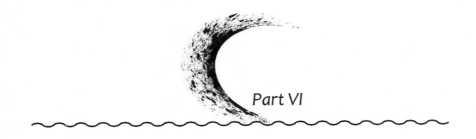

Part VI

Back to September

Twenty-Five

Joe didn't know that while people were enjoying the Eagle Festival, and while he was narrowly avoiding being killed, every local and state OSR, as well as every state militia, received an update on messages they had been receiving regularly for the past several weeks.

Wildfires in California, Arizona, Colorado, and Washington State are on the increase. Crews are not able to snuff them out. Many people have been killed, more displaced. Hundreds of homes burned. Thousands of acres of profitable forest land were destroyed. Flames and smoke are high into the air, spreading across the region.

Flooding on the East Coast continues. New Jersey is essentially claimed by the Atlantic Ocean, as well as much of New York City, Boston, and all other coastal cities and towns. All of Florida, except the Panhandle, is now completely underwater and lost. The state of Georgia is overwhelmed with displaced people trying to escape the floods.

Of course these messages never reached the public, and unless they were directly affected, as thousands of people in the coastal regions and in the West were, most people did not know about the devastating ravages happening around the country: droughts, storms, and ocean flooding. The daily digital *National Eagle Reporter* that everyone received on their SPEDs continued with its regular menu of insipid material.

We trust everyone is enjoying these early fall days, with the occasional rains. It is invigorating weather. Just a wonderful time to be alive.

The usual "inspiring" message followed: *Those who respect authority will succeed.*

In reality, the federal Office for Social Responsibility and Department of Homeland Security were in turmoil, completely overwhelmed by weather emergencies around the country. In mid-September both federal offices received an emergency message from the National Weather Company, which was responsible for compiling information from the many local weather companies scattered across the country.

East Coast weather companies are predicting a monster storm to hit the East Coast in twenty-four hours. Strong winds from the northeast will collide with warm moist air from the Gulf of Mexico and cool air from Canada flowing east to create the storm. Winds are predicted to be up to two hundred miles per hour. Rainfall could exceed two inches per hour. Storm surges will cause further flooding on the East Coast. Storm is expected to maintain strength as it moves west, causing havoc to the interior states. Flooding around the Great Lakes is likely.

Federal OSR officials debated sending this new storm information to the local OSRs, especially in northeast Wisconsin, where the storm was likely to make a direct hit. One official said, "They've got enough worries out there in the hinterland. They don't need one more piece of bad news." And the message was not sent.

Back in Crystal River, Andy and Liz received the coded message about a killer storm from Andy's brother, Herman. His coded message had put them on high alert. A strong storm rolled through their area after they went to bed that night, and they anxiously awaited news about what was happening up in Door County. The next day, Andy's SPED buzzed. Andy immediately noted that the message was from Herman and it was not coded.

Andy,

Devastation here. I'm in Sturgeon Bay, trying to travel to Crystal River. I caught a ride with a person from Chicago. Hundreds of people are walking. The roads are lined with men, women, and children, all walking south. Tourists' cars, most with Illinois license plates, are backed up for miles on both Highways 42 and 57. Much of Highway 57 is washed out. I just heard from someone who said several hundred people traveling on 57 were washed into Lake Michigan and likely drowned. Both bridges in Sturgeon Bay are gone, washed away.

The only way out now is by boat. Rain is still pouring down in sheets. Never saw a storm like this. We just passed a young woman lying alongside the road, clutching a young child. Both appeared dead, but nobody stopped to check. Everyone is in a panic. We are moving south as best we can.

Much of Door County is gone. All of Washington Island is lost. I heard from a fellow traveler that ferry boats trying to remove people from the island sank in Death's Door, the passageway to the mainland, with no survivors. Never in my long life have I seen such a calamity. The local militia are nowhere in sight. I heard that they were the first to leave the county, along with those working in the OSR.

I hope to make it to your place, Andy. Pray for me. Pray for the people of Door County. The smell of death is everywhere. Let people know what's happening here.

Herman

Andy read the message, and then he read it a second time. *How can I let people know?* he thought, panic rising. He guessed the local OSR had surely read this message, as they read all messages. *I wonder if they knew it was coming. Such devastation and death,* thought Andy. The OSR was reluctant to share bad news, no matter how terrible it was.

All Andy Schmidt could think about that afternoon was his brother. Liz told him that if Herman was anything like Andy, he would survive. She didn't need to remind Andy that Herman was sixty-five years old.

The stream of displaced persons escaping the devastated Door County reached twenty thousand people, the estimate that the Door County Office for Social Responsibility reported on their communication link to the Wisconsin State Militia Office in Madison and to the local OSR offices located around the state. Of course the Door County OSR did not mention that its staff was the first to leave the county. They hurried to set up temporary offices on high ground south of Green Bay.

Wisconsin's militia, trying to respond to the disaster as best they could, sent army trucks left over from the old wars to haul people to disaster centers, which were quickly established in the former state and local parks, now all privately owned. The parks were informed by the state OSR that they would be receiving displaced citizens and should be prepared for their arrival. No mention was made as to how long they were expected to stay. The national Homeland Security department, acting on direct orders from President John Emery, began sending army tents, combat rations, and other survival equipment to Wisconsin.

President Emery's office had been battered for months, thanks to its inadequate response to the floods on the East and West coasts, the devastation in Florida, the wildfires in the Northwest, and the continuing drought in the Southwest. In his eighteen years in office, the president had never gotten such negative reactions from around the country, and he knew that his office and the federal agencies responsible for challenges like this had to do a better job. He was also well aware that his administration's attempt to keep bad news away from all citizens hadn't worked. After being told for so long that climate change was a hoax and something to be ignored, people were experiencing its devastating effects firsthand.

Emery's office sent a message to the SPED of every Wisconsin resident:

I know about the terrible loss the people of Door County have faced—loss of homes, loss of businesses, and unfortunately even loss of life. Everyone in my administration is thinking about the people of Wisconsin and what you are facing. We know that you will do everything you can to assist the twenty thousand people who have had to leave their beloved county, with no hope of returning, as I'm told most of Door County has been destroyed by high winds, torrential rains, and associated flooding. We are relocating the displaced people in parks and other suitable places where they will be provided food and shelter until other arrangements can be made for them.

I have asked my Department of Homeland Security to assist your state militia in any way it can. Likewise, I've instructed the local Offices of Social Responsibility to help people using all the resources they have available.

The local OSRs and the Wisconsin State Militia Office received their own message, one only they could see. It read:

Don't screw up this Door County deal. Once these people get over the shock of what's happened to them, they'll want results. Do whatever you can to keep them from complaining. Give them minimum aid. We've got problems in other parts of the country, as you well know. If the Eagle Party is to keep its place as a leader in creating a moral society—our ultimate goal—we must keep people under control. I know you will do your best. John Emery, President of the United States.

Twenty-Six

All day long Liz and Andy worked in their garden and watched old camouflaged army trucks spewing black diesel fumes pass by. Dust swirled around the sputtering old trucks as they carried haggard and exhausted men, women, and children to their destination in the former Pioneer State Park, located just outside Crystal River. They sat in the open backs of the trucks, the dust often making them invisible to anyone watching them move by. Many of the hungry and tired Door County refugees clutched garbage bags filled with a few meager belongings that they had quickly grabbed before the winds and floods sent them scurrying to safety, like rats deserting a sinking ship.

They were on their way to the former Pioneer State Park, now known as Happy Valley Park. Neither Liz nor Andy had visited the park since it had been sold by the state. They couldn't afford the high fees.

Liz heard her SPED buzz and she looked down. It was a message from Tracy Smith, head of the regional Office for Social Responsibility—an office that she never wanted to hear from. And at this moment, she feared the message had to do with the OSR learning that the Oldsters were not the people that everyone thought they were, but were in fact trying to create a social revolution. But she was surprised at what she read:

To Liz Carall, president, Crystal River Oldsters.

You may have noticed army trucks traveling through your town. They are transporting some one thousand men, women, and children to Happy Valley Park. These are displaced persons from the devastation that has recently befallen Door County.

I know that the Oldsters have made many fine contributions to the Crystal River community, and I am asking if you and members of your organization would be willing to help our local militia and our local OSR provide these displaced people with what they will need to survive. Can you help us?

Liz, more than surprised, shared the information with Andy. "I'm thinking we should do something," said Liz, "just in case some governmental officials believe we've been up to no good." She smiled when she said it. "I think I'll call an emergency meeting of the Oldsters to discuss this."

She immediately sent a message to the Crystal River Oldster members: *Emergency meeting. Tomorrow at 10 a.m.*

The first thing Liz noticed when she entered the Last Chapter Saloon was no special greeting from Bill. She would miss the friendly bartender, who had seemed to enjoy talking to everyone who came through the Last Chapter's door.

Liz called the meeting to order and, as always, checked first with John Owens to confirm that he had disabled the listening device. Then she began. "You all read the message from President Emery about the devastation in Door County and the thousands of people who have been displaced. You've also likely seen the army trucks rolling through town, loaded with men, women, and children, headed for Happy Valley Park." Heads were nodding in agreement. "What you probably don't know is that about a thousand people are now at the park."

Liz explained the message from Tracy Smith at the regional OSR. "She sounded desperate," Liz said. "Between the OSR and the local militia there simply are not enough resources to take care of the nearly twenty thousand displaced people. She is asking if we will volunteer to help the thousand or so who were transported by army trucks to Happy Valley Park."

"Why should we help the OSR?" a former Crystal River business-woman asked. She had owned and operated a women's clothing store that carried high-quality but fairly expensive clothing. Her business had died when all but a handful of women could afford to buy what she had to sell. "It's because of that blasted Eagle Party that this country is in the fix it is," she said. They created this problem—remember, they're the ones who said just forget about climate change, and figure out how to get rich. Let them deal with it."

Several other Oldster members nodded their heads in agreement.

A member who had been a nurse and seldom said anything at the Oldster meetings but always attended held up her hand. "As most of you know, I worked as a nurse for thirty-five years," she said. "My job was to help people in need, the poor as well as the rich. My vote is to help these people. It is not their fault that they face this most difficult time in their lives."

The discussion went on for an hour, with several people speaking in favor and a similar number disagreeing.

After listening to both sides of the argument, Liz finally broke in. "I have an idea," she began. "I understand the reluctance for many of you to help the OSR. And I also have great respect for those who want, no matter the circumstances, to help those in need. But here's my idea—a bit far out perhaps, but I think it is worth a try." She stopped talking and looked around the room. Everyone was looking in her direction, and those who had been whispering to each other now looked up to hear what she had to say.

"First, I propose we accept the invitation from the regional OSR to volunteer our services at the park." Several groans came from the audience.

"Hold on, let me finish," Liz said, holding up a hand. "I propose that we help this group of displaced people and while we are doing it, show them how to become a self-supporting, democratically run community. That we put into practice, through a 'learning by doing' approach, everything that we've been trying to do in the schools. I suggest we offer learning opportunities for young and old and we help the refugees elect their own leaders and decide how they want to run their community."

The room was quiet. People were thinking. "Then," Liz said, "we will let the country know what this one community is doing, and how they are doing it." She continued loudly and with passion. "We Oldsters are not done yet. This may be our chance. This may be our opportunity to do the things we've struggled to do. It's a time when the entire Eagle Party administration has its hands full with all the devastation going on in this country and might not have time to check up on us. By the way, did any of you notice that no drones were flying this morning?"

Several hands went up.

"I think it's time for a vote," said Andy.

"Okay, all in favor of volunteering at the park, raise your hands. Andy, you and John count," Liz said.

Hands went up and the two men recorded the count.

"Those who are opposed, raise your hands."

John and Andy counted.

Liz looked to John for the results.

"Andy and I count thirty in favor, four opposed, and one person not voting."

"Thank you," said Liz. "I will let the regional OSR know of our plans."

As people were leaving, Liz sat off to the side, working on her SPED, sending a message to Tracy Smith.

The Crystal River Oldsters will volunteer to help at Happy Valley Park. How should we proceed? Liz.

Twenty-Seven

Before Liz Carall left the meeting room, her SPED buzzed. She looked at it and read:

> Liz: Thank you. When you arrive at the park gate, mention my name and that you are volunteers there to help Door County people. Tracy.

What an ironic switch, thought Liz. *I'm now on a first-name basis with the OSR director, who, if she knew who we really were, would have us abolished.* Then it occurred to Liz: *Maybe they know all about us and have no choice but to ask for our help.*

She also wondered if the Office for Social Responsibility would indeed be so busy with other challenges that they would leave them alone with the Door County people and not try to monitor their efforts. Liz was well aware that the OSR drones had ceased flying several days ago—that was a good sign.

Liz had seen so many disappointments, starting with her dismissal from Badger State University and followed by the setbacks in her various ideas for infiltrating the schools and universities with Oldster Associates. The destruction of Onthaway Academy was the most serious setback, for the Oldsters now had no place to train their associates. Liz had been about to give up all that she had hoped that the Oldsters could accomplish. It was clearly a cold-as-thunder time for her. But then came the devastating storm that destroyed one of Wisconsin's most beautiful counties. Liz thought, *Is this the opportunity I've been waiting for? Will it be possible for something good to come from something so devastating, so awful?*

Upon arriving back home, Liz took out her SPED and sent a message to the Crystal River Oldsters, asking them to meet at the park entrance the following morning promptly at eight.

That evening, after Liz and Andy were in bed, a quiet knock on their door awakened them. Andy got up, pulled on his pants, and in bare feet stumbled in the dark to the door. He opened it to see his brother, Herman, standing there, shirt torn, gray hair a tangled mess.

"Can I come in?" Herman said quietly.

"Yes, yes, come in, come in," said Andy, overjoyed to see his brother.

The two men hugged for a long time before Andy said, "Liz, it's Herman, he made it."

Liz was soon up, brewing a pot of coffee and making sandwiches for Herman, who had not eaten for two days. The three of them sat at the old farmhouse's kitchen table, the same one that had been in that very spot when Andy and Herman were boys. Herman told, in gruesome detail, of the death and destruction in what had been his home for so many years. With tears in his eyes he described the sight of children who had drowned and washed up on the shores of Lake Michigan after they had tried to escape the total destruction of Washington Island off the tip of Door County. He recounted how most of the homes and businesses in his beloved Baileys Harbor had washed into Lake Michigan, in some cases with people still inside, their screams heard over the driving rain and high wind.

Finally, Herman admitted that he hadn't slept for forty-eight hours, and asked if they had a spare bed.

"Of course we do," said Liz, showing the exhausted man to a bed, where he collapsed without taking off his clothes.

The following morning, Liz arrived at the entrance to Happy Valley Park and encountered a sleepy state militia sentry, squinting into the sun. He wore a camouflaged uniform and helmet and he had an automatic weapon.

It was a beautiful September day, temperature in the seventies, with a cool breeze blowing from the west.

"The park is closed," the sentry said as he removed his weapon from his shoulder and held it in front of him. "Please leave."

As he spoke, other Oldster members began arriving.

"We have permission from Tracy Smith, the regional OSR director, to be here," Liz said.

"Never heard of her," said the sentry, looking anxious now that some thirty-five people had gathered in front of him. "The park is closed," he repeated.

"Could you check with someone, please? We're ready to go to work," said Liz.

"To do what?" the sentry asked. "There's no work here."

"Could you please check with your superior?"

"He doesn't want to be bothered this early in the morning," the sentry said. Liz could see that he was beginning to perspire as the Oldsters pressed in closer to hear the discussion Liz was having with him.

The sentry slipped his automatic rifle back over his shoulder and fished his SPED from his pocket, pushed a button, and said, "Captain, there's a bunch of old people out here telling me they've come to work. The head old lady said she had gotten permission from Tracy somebody with the OSR. Know anything about this?"

The sentry listened carefully and then stuffed his SPED back in his pocket.

"You can go in," he said gruffly. "Stop at the headquarters building and report to Captain Grassley before you go anywhere. But be careful. Can't trust them folks we hauled in here from Door County. Yesterday I was watching over a bunch of them lined up for water. This young guy at the back of the line crowded up toward the front. I told him to get back in line, but he said his sister was sick and needed water. He refused to move so I gave him a whack with the butt of my rifle. Taught him a lesson. So you folks watch out. There ain't enough of us militia here to protect you."

He proceeded to lift the gate that allowed the Oldsters to enter the park.

"Thank you," Liz said. She had wanted to say more, to tell this guy that he had been out of line. But she knew better and even wondered if he might try to teach her a lesson with the butt of his rifle.

As Liz and her fellow Oldsters walked into the park, she remembered the fun times she had there when she was a kid and the park was known as Pioneer State Park. She remembered seeing men with horses working in the fields, showing everyone what farm life had been in the early 1900s. She remembered the smell of freshly worked soil, and the squeaky sound of horse leather as a team of Belgians—that's what her father told her they were—strained into their harnesses as the man with the plow struggled along behind, sweat beading on his forehead. She especially remembered the pungent smell of horse sweat as the team moved by, turning over a ribbon of black soil.

She had not been in the park since it had been sold and the entry fees had increased. And apparently the wealthy had not visited in sufficient numbers for the company that now owned the place to keep it in good repair. As she and her fellow Oldsters walked along the dusty path leading toward a cluster of tents, she saw that the grass had not been cut all summer. Brush and berry vines hung heavy over the walkway, and a huge old oak tree had toppled across the path. No apparent attempt had been made to remove it. She could see where the army trucks carrying the refugees had driven around it.

They crossed the rickety wooden bridge over the Crystal River that flowed through the park. The river appeared cleaner and less strewn with trash compared to where it flowed through the Town of Crystal River. When they reached what had been the park headquarters building, she saw a hastily made sign over the big wooden door: HQ Wisconsin Militia, Company 12. She opened the door and immediately remembered the good times she and her family had in this big room, when a rainstorm had come up and they sought shelter there, or where, on a cool fall day, they had gathered in front of the big fireplace at one end of the room to enjoy the warmth and the quiet. She saw a door marked Office. She knocked and heard, "Enter." She opened the door and saw a man in uniform sitting behind a desk cluttered with papers. Behind him was an open door leading to an interior office.

"You must represent this Oldster group that's here to help."

"Yes," said Liz. "I'm supposed to report to Captain Grassley."

Hearing his name, a tall, thin, balding middle-aged man appeared.

"I'm Captain George Grassley," the man said in a pleasant voice. "Sorry for the mix-up. Our sentry at the gate apparently didn't read his daily orders. And you are?" the officer asked.

"I'm Liz. Liz Carall. I'm president of the Crystal River Oldsters. We're a group of retired people and we're here to help."

Liz thrust out her hand and Grassley shook it. He had a firm handshake. She wondered what he did when he wasn't on active duty with the militia.

"I'm pleased that your group has volunteered to give us a hand," Grassley said. "There are only fifty of us here, and we're about overwhelmed. We've got about a thousand people we're trying to take care of—and to be perfectly honest about it, none of us has had any training dealing with displaced persons."

"We'll see what we can do," said Liz, surprised at the apparent humanity of this man in contrast to the sentry she had encountered at the gate.

"We need help distributing rations, we need help getting water to these people, and frankly, for some of them, they just need to talk to someone and calm down. The fact that they have lost most of what they owned has just dawned on some of these folks. Quite a few also lost loved ones, spouses, children, and they are grieving." The man shook his head, obviously struck by the weight of his assignment.

As Liz turned to leave, the officer shook Liz's hand once more and looked straight at her. She noticed that he had deep-blue eyes. "Thank you," he said. "Thank you and your members. You are lifesavers."

As Liz left the tiny office and walked outside, she thought, *How could this caring man be a part of such an uncaring group of people and continue to hold his job, even survive?*

She beckoned to the waiting Oldsters, and they proceeded to the entryway to what had become an enormous tent city.

"What are you all doing here?" the sentry asked. He, like his colleague at the main gate, was in full military uniform, complete with an automatic weapon. And he apparently had not read his daily orders either.

Liz explained that she had just talked to his commanding officer, and that they had been asked to help the displaced people in any way they could.

"Don't know that they need any help," the sentry said. "But you all look harmless enough, so go on in."

State OSR director Fred Putkey relaxed a bit when he got Bill's message that Joe had been eliminated. Of course he had no way of knowing that it really was Bill who was killed and Joe was very much alive. When he received the message, Putkey thought, *One less problem to think about.* It was only a few weeks later that the devastating storm struck Door County. His office had been incredibly busy and he didn't have time to think about anything else, such as what was going on with the Crystal River Oldsters.

The OSR and the militia had successfully found temporary shelter for the twenty thousand displaced people, assigning about a thousand to each of twenty former state parks that the OSR had taken over from their private owners.

Putkey had been hearing from most of the park owners with some version of the following: "When do you plan for these people to leave my park? The militia is keeping all visitors away."

"Soon," Putkey would reply. In reality he had no idea about what to do next with all the displaced people. The state militia was doing what it could by providing tents, water, and emergency rations, and trying to keep some measure of control at the parks while keeping people away, especially those who wanted to see what a displaced-person camp looked like.

He thought back to Bill and the Crystal River situation and wondered how he should proceed. Perhaps he should let Tracy Smith at the regional office know what he had learned about the local Oldsters and what steps he had taken to solve the problem. It was not his style to do that; the fewer people who knew about such matters, the better. Then his SPED buzzed again with yet another message from a park owner: "Get rid of these people. They are bad for business."

Twenty-Eight

Liz divided the Oldsters in teams of two to walk among the tents; count the men, women, and children; and talk with the people, get to know them a little, and inform them that the Oldsters were there to help them in any way possible. She assigned each team several rows of tents.

Liz teamed up with Pastor Larry and they began walking from tent to tent.

"Anybody home?" Liz asked as they approached a faded old tent with US Army printed on the flap. A little blonde girl peaked out to see who was there.

"What is your name?" asked Liz. The little girl had a dirty face and wore a torn dress.

"I'm Jenny," said the girl.

"I'm Liz, and this is Larry," Liz said, holding out her hand to the little girl. "Is your daddy here?"

"No, he went looking for water. We're all so thirsty, and it's a long walk to the water truck. It was empty yesterday when Daddy went for water. We're all so thirsty."

"Is your mommy here?"

"She's nursing my baby brother."

"Have you had something to eat?" Pastor Larry asked.

"Yes, but it was bad. Old tasting. Couldn't even tell what it was. But we were so hungry. Mommy has been crying. She can't stop crying," the little girl said, brushing away both a tear and some blonde hair that had fallen over her face. "When can we go home? I don't like it here. These army men are mean. Why do they have to be so mean?" The little girl began sobbing, her whole body shaking. Liz grabbed her up, hugged her, and held her close.

"We're here to help you," was all she could think to say.

"I just want to go home," the little girl said as she turned, opened the tent flap, and disappeared into the inside of the dark, windowless tent. Standing in front of the tent, Liz and Pastor Larry could smell the musty scent of canvas that had been in storage for years.

Pastor Larry carried a pad of paper and on it he wrote: *1 man, 1 woman (nursing), 1 infant, and 1 little girl, approximate age 8 years.*

They walked to the next tent, where a sullen-faced man with a three-day growth of black whiskers sat on a block of wood, holding his face in his hands.

"Hello," Pastor Larry said as he and Liz approached. The man looked up; his eyes were red and he looked like he had not slept for days.

"I'm Larry and this is Liz," said Pastor Larry. "We are members of the Crystal River Oldsters and are here to help in any way we can."

"Help, huh? Well, I hope you got more to offer than those yahoo militia guys who strut around here waving their guns and looking like they own the place," the man said, spitting out the words.

"We have nothing to do with the militia. We are a group of retired volunteers."

"Right. So what have you got to offer?" the man asked defiantly.

"Well, tell us what you need. Let's start with that."

"First off, if you could find my wife . . ." He hesitated. "If you could find my wife . . . She's been missing since the flood." Now he brushed a dirty hand across his eyes. "She's missing and we've got three kids to take care of. Find my wife. That's how you can help. Find out if she's here. Find out if she made it out. I've been looking for two days. Looking for two days." The man sat down and began sobbing.

Pastor Larry put his arm around the man. "What's your wife's name?"

"It's Jody," he said, hesitantly. "Jody Carlson."

"We'll see what we can do. Oldster members are visiting all the tents. If she's here, we'll find her."

"Thank you," the man said. "And God bless you."

Surprised to hear words he had not heard in years, he said to the man, "I will pray for you."

"Thank you," the man said. "Thank you." He grabbed Pastor Larry's hand and shook it vigorously.

Walking away, Pastor Larry wrote on his pad: *father, 3 children, ages unknown, mother Jody Carlson missing since flood.*

The third tent was tightly closed, even on this quickly warming September day.

"Knock, knock," Liz said quietly as she and Pastor Larry stood in front of the structure.

"Go away," a woman's husky voice said from inside. "Leave us alone. Haven't you done enough to us already? Just go away."

"Can we talk to you?" asked Liz. "We're not the militia. We are here to help you."

"We don't need no damn help. Just leave. If you want to help, make the floods go away so we can go home," the woman said sarcastically.

Pastor Larry wrote on his pad: *1 woman, 1 other person not identified.*

At the next tent, somebody was cooking something over a little open fire.

"Hello," Liz said. "How are you?"

"We're blessed, truly blessed," the woman said. "We almost drowned, my husband and I, but here we are, alive and well. With a roof over our heads, sort of." She smiled when she said it. "Something to eat and no water lapping at our ankles. Truly blessed we are."

"This is Larry and I'm Liz. We are members of the Crystal River Oldsters, here to help you folks in any way we can."

"So far so good," the woman said as she stirred something in the pot, the smell of her cooking drifting across the tent city. "So far so good."

Late that afternoon, after the Oldsters had completed their survey of the refugees, Liz called an evening meeting of the Oldsters at the Last Chapter Saloon.

Liz asked those who had walked among the tents for the statistics. They had counted 975 people. Of the total, 150 were men, 145 women, 300 children four and younger, 200 children five to twelve, and 180 young people ages thirteen to seventeen.

"We must be most concerned about the kids four and younger," she said. Next she asked what they had learned from talking with the people. It was mostly in line with what she and Pastor Larry had heard. Almost everyone reported some reference to religion. Many of the adults remembered how important their church had been to them, and now, in their time of great need, they hoped that people were praying for them.

Liz asked, "How many of the people you talked with mentioned the name of someone missing?"

Several Oldsters raised their hands.

"We should make a list of the names of those missing and post it at the headquarters building, just in case the missing persons got separated from their families but are elsewhere in the camp," Liz suggested.

"I'll do it," offered Pastor Larry.

"One thing I learned from talking with the refugees is that some of them simply can't accept that they've lost everything and must start over," said Joe Vogel, who had been one of those helping with the assessment. Joe, even though he had taken care of the problem with Bill the bartender, was still feeling a bit paranoid. Would someone show up at any moment and recognize who he really was and disrupt the surprisingly contented life he had created for himself in Crystal River? He was relieved to put the OSR behind him, and he would do just about anything to protect his new life, even though it meant not telling anyone of his true identity.

The discussion went on for nearly an hour. Liz thanked everyone and said she hoped they would have time to continue volunteering at the park. "I suggest we work diligently for the next two weeks, helping the militia in any way we can and gaining their trust while at the same time gaining the trust of the displaced people. At the end of two weeks, I want to try something. I don't want to get your hopes up, but here's what I want to try." She went on to explain her new plan in detail. *This just might work*, she thought.

Twenty-Nine

The Oldster volunteers spent the next two weeks carrying water, distributing food, talking with people, and listening to their concerns. On a cool, late September morning, Liz Carall stopped at the militia office to talk with Captain Grassley.

"Have a chair," said Grassley as he welcomed her into his office. "Thanks for stopping by, and thanks to you and your Oldster group. Everything is going quite well, especially considering where we were a couple of weeks ago. I just got a report from Tracy Smith, the regional director for the OSR. As you know she stopped by for an inspection tour last week."

"Yes, I showed her around," said Liz, glad that Grassley didn't know how she had picked and chosen what Tracy should see and with whom she should talk.

"There's a reason for my visit," began Liz. "I know how overworked the Wisconsin militia is these days with the displaced Door County people scattered around the state at various parks." She hesitated before going on, trying to read Captain Grassley's reaction.

"It's true. We've got just about all we can handle, and the national Homeland Security people and the Offices of Social Responsibility have their hands full dealing with the calamities in other parts of the country."

"Here's what I want to offer," said Liz. "Turn the management of this park over to our Oldster group and let us be in charge. We've been here long enough to know what to do. Leave us a good supply of rations, the tents, and your water trucks, and we'll take over."

Without hesitating for a moment, Grassley said, "Are you sure you can handle it? Some of these people are a little unstable; some may even be violent. And none of them want to be here."

Liz and her fellow Oldsters had gotten to know the refugees quite well, and true, a few of them seemed a little unhinged after all they had been through, and some were having difficulty accepting their situation, but she didn't believe anyone was violent.

"I think we can handle it," said Liz confidently.

"Well, it sounds like a good idea to me. I sure wouldn't mind leaving this place. My family hasn't seen me in nearly three weeks." He got up from behind his desk and looked out the little office window toward the rows of old army tents stretching nearly as far as he could see.

He turned back to Liz. "I'll have to check with my commander in Milwaukee to see what he thinks, and I'll get back to you tomorrow. And thanks for the offer. It's the best thing I've heard since I got here."

Not fifteen minutes after Liz arrived home, her SPED buzzed. She read the following message:

To: Liz Carall

Your proposal has been accepted, with my personal thanks. My troopers and I will plan to leave a week from today, and the place will be all yours. I will make sure that what you asked for from us will be available. Thank you again.

George Grassley, Captain, Wisconsin Militia

Unhappy messages from park owners housing the displaced persons from Door County continued to pour into the Wisconsin Office for Social Responsibility, which had overall supervision of the refugee crisis in the parks. Fred Putkey, reluctant to contact the federal office because it might show leadership weakness, finally sent a terse message to Washington, asking for advice as to how he should deal with the twenty irate park owners who, to a person, were demanding that the refugees be forcibly removed from their parks. He received this message:

Putkey was both relieved and concerned. He was glad that a decision had been made and that he didn't have to worry about what to do with twenty thousand people because they could now stay in the parks indefinitely. But he was concerned the park owners would become one more group that would be alienated because of the current administration's heavy-handed tactics and that would likely result in their diminished support for the Eagle Party.

Putkey received two other messages, one from Tracy Smith, commending the Crystal River Oldsters for assisting the militia at Happy Valley Park, and the most recent one, a copy of a message from the militia captain at Happy Valley saying he was turning over operations of the refugee camp to the Crystal River Oldsters.

He was surprised and pleased. This was confirmation that Bill the bartender at the Last Chapter Saloon had obviously done his job and eliminated the turncoat, Joe Vogel, and turned the Crystal River Oldsters in the right direction of supporting the Eagle Party with its limited resources.

Putkey sat back in his chair and relaxed for the first time since the disaster in Door County had occurred.

A week later, Liz and her band of Oldsters arrived at Happy Valley Park in time to see a pair of militia troopers taking down the company headquarters sign while Captain Grassley watched.

"The last truck is about to leave," Grassley said when he saw Liz walking toward the former park headquarters. "The water trucks are parked out back; the food is stored where you've found it previously. And the place is yours. Oh, you should also know that the federal government has taken over ownership of all parks housing refugees. The refugees can stay here as long as they want, but they will have to figure out how to do it." He extended his hand to Liz. "Thank you. Your gracious offer is very much appreciated." He turned and climbed into the front of the truck, which had several troopers riding in the back. The old diesel army truck roared on down the dusty road, across the wooden bridge spanning the Crystal River, and was soon out of sight.

Liz turned in the direction of the tent city. She heard loud cheering and clapping and saw the men, women, and children standing in front of their tents. She hoped that they would continue to cheer her and the other Oldsters when they began introducing their new ideas.

She turned back to the Oldsters. "First, I need a volunteer Oldster to organize our security, to make sure nobody comes visiting who shouldn't be here." A hand went up at the back.

"Joe Vogel," Liz said. She almost didn't recognize him, as he had grown a bushy beard and wore dark glasses.

"I'll do it," Joe said as he walked to the front of the group. He had learned that three Oldster men had served in the state militia, but the only action they had seen was helping with flood control several decades earlier. He knew he had more military training, particularly combat training, than anyone in the group.

"Thank you, Joe," Liz said. "There's a good fence around this park, but I want you to organize a cadre of sentries to make sure no one comes into this place without our permission." Joe smiled to himself. He was the one person who knew military tactics. He was also the only one who had firearms, but he kept them secretly hidden and hoped to continue to do so. Joe immediately began thinking about which men among the refugees he would ask to help him with sentry duties.

Liz was smiling too as she walked toward the cheering crowd of refugees. She knew that the Oldsters were making real progress toward their goals. But she wondered if her ideas, which had resulted in lukewarm success in the past, would really work this time. Learning that the refugees could stay in the park indefinitely was good news. But the way that the federal government had handled the situation disturbed Liz. Would the former park owner come calling with the intention of reclaiming the property that he believed was rightfully his? She must let Joe and his sentries know that there may be trouble down the road.

Thirty

After the last truck left, Liz, followed by the Oldster volunteers, entered the massive tent city with its clapping and cheering residents.

"Thank you," Liz said, using a portable, solar-powered sound amplifier that the militia had left behind. "As you likely know, the militia has gone. They have gone for good." More cheering and clapping followed. "There is more good news. You will be able to stay here as long as you want." For this there was less cheering, as many were hoping for better living conditions than a tent and surplus army emergency rations, especially with winter but a few months away. Everyone knew about Wisconsin winters, which could still be harsh, even as the region's climate had been growing warmer.

"Some of you may wish to leave, and that is your right. But for those of you who plan to stay, we believe we have something to offer that you will appreciate. At one o'clock today, I would like to meet all of you at what was once the park's amphitheater. You all know where it is, on that little hill that runs down to the Crystal River." She pointed in the direction of the amphitheater with its rows of stone benches that had, according to a brass plaque screwed in to the amphitheater's stone wall, been constructed by the Civilian Conservation Corps back in the 1930s.

"I hope to see you all then," Liz said.

Putting down the voice amplifier, she said to her fellow Oldsters, "Let's meet at park headquarters in fifteen minutes."

When the Oldsters were all assembled and seated in the big room at park headquarters, Liz said, "Well, we've got our work cut out for us. This is the opportunity we've been waiting for. But it will be an enormous challenge. We have the opportunity to help these refugees become a self-sustaining community, and to become a model for others who wish to take control of their own destinies rather than constantly suffer under the thumb of the oppressive government that now runs this country.

"Our schools and especially our government have everyone believing that a select group, those with power and money, will take care of us and protect us from harm, and for this security we must give up our liberty and our right to decide our own destinies. Our first task is to help them realize what they can do for themselves by cooperating, rather than always competing, as many of them were taught was the only way to prosper."

The Oldsters clapped when Liz finished her little impassioned speech. Everyone agreed with what Liz was saying, and they were as frustrated as she was about the progress the Oldsters had made in Crystal River and throughout the Upper Midwest. Since the destruction of Onthaway Academy, several of the Oldster chapters had given up, admitted defeat, and decided to knuckle under the control of their local Offices of Social Responsibility.

Looking toward her husband, Liz said, "Andy, we'll need you to explain to the displaced people what you told me you learned in college about the elements of an ideal rural community."

Then she turned to Pastor Larry. "Larry, you and I have talked about this. You'll work with those who are religious and want to continue practicing their faith."

She looked at John Owens. "John, you mentioned to me your interest in bartering systems—could we make that work here?" John nodded without hesitation.

"And Emily," Liz continued, "with your years as an English teacher and writing instructor, you will think of ways to involve folks in writing projects that will help them explore their histories and where they are now in their lives."

An older Oldster, who never said much, now looked at Liz and said, "All this sounds mighty dangerous. What if the OSR people find out what we're doing is much more than distributing old army rations and patching holes in leaky tents?"

"So far we are on the good side of OSR. In fact, we've been commended for what we've done so far," answered Liz. "But you're right. We have to be careful. Especially if they begin flying those dreaded drones once more. I haven't seen one in several weeks, and I'm hoping I won't see any. We also plan to keep a guard at the park's entrance gate at all times, and we'll patrol the fence to make sure nobody sneaks in and finds out what we're doing."

When the refugees all assembled at the amphitheater, Liz spoke into the voice amplifier, thanking everyone for coming. She wondered how many families had chosen to leave, but she was encouraged to see what she believed to be most of the displaced people in attendance.

She asked, "How many of you have no other place to go, no other place to live?" All the hands went up.

"Okay, let's get down to the basics. Winter is but a few months away, and we've got to plan for more permanent housing than these drafty old army tents. We need alternatives. We've got enough emergency food rations to last several months, but we've got to plan for food. Water should not be a problem. The well here is powered by a solar generator and the militia left us their water trucks."

As the refugees took in the fact that the Oldsters were concerned about first helping them provide for their basic needs, they seemed to relax. Liz even noticed a few smiles.

"We'll make some suggestions, but you've got to do it yourselves," she continued. "Andy, will you show us a way to do it?"

Andy Schmidt took the amplifier from Liz and began, "Here are some ideas I got from a course I took in college many years ago." He smiled when he said it. "I thought the ideas were good then, and I believe they are still good today. The course was called 'How to Organize an Ideal Rural Community.' Here goes." Andy began by explaining that the park had once been farmland. It consisted of five hundred acres, about one hundred acres of it wooded.

"My idea is for you to figure out how to create a village, with permanent houses and access to about three hundred acres of land, where you can grow vegetables and other crops. Each family would have its own home, but you would work the land together and likewise share the crops that you grow."

Several hands shot up. "Yes?" Andy said to the first person holding up a hand.

"I don't think there are twenty farmers among us," the man said. "I ran a motel in Baileys Harbor. I know nothing about farming."

"We'll help you," Andy said. "Those of us who know how will help you." He continued. "Based on the count we did and considering that a few families have chosen to leave, there are about 250 adult men and women in this group. I suggest you divide yourselves into fifteen groups with about fifteen to twenty people in each group. Discuss your preference for where to locate the village. Then select one person from your little group to be its spokesperson."

The refugees appeared stunned. It had been such a long time since they had done anything remotely like this, and many of the younger people never had. In fact, activities like this had been strongly discouraged. The OSR would punish those who got together to make decisions about anything. They looked at each other, wondering whom to form groups with.

"I suggest you talk among yourselves this afternoon and this evening and organize the groups. Tomorrow, I'll meet with the spokespeople. Feel free to stop by the park headquarters building, where I've posted on the wall a sample design for a village with open farmland behind it to give you a visual picture of what we're suggesting. One more thing. Many of you probably still have your SPEDs. Please don't use them. We don't know who might be listening and reading what you say. We would all be in danger if the government learned what we are planning to do here."

Liz Carall stood to the side, smiling. *They're all listening to what Andy has to say*, she thought. She was concerned that people had been so brainwashed by what they had seen and heard from the Eagle Party for the last sixteen years that the idea of making their own decisions would be so foreign that they would reject it. But so far so good.

Thirty-One

When the Oldsters returned to the park the following morning, Liz and Andy stopped by the park headquarters building and saw eight women and seven men waiting for them. All were smiling and apparently having a good time chatting with each other.

"Well," Andy began, "my guess is that you folks are the spokespeople from your groups."

"We are," said a smiling young woman, obviously pleased that she had been selected to represent her group.

"Have you decided where to locate the village?" asked Andy.

"Yes, we have. We want the village to have access to both the river and the farmland. We've agreed on a potential site."

An older gentleman held up his hand. "I must speak up," he began. He was rubbing his whisker-covered chin. "I think this whole idea is dumb, dumb, dumb. Why do we screw around trying to build a village? What we ought to do is get after the OSR and the Eagle Party people in Washington and here in Wisconsin and find out what they have in mind for us. They took care of us in the past; why can't we expect them to take care of us in the future? These tents ain't all that bad. And so far we've got something to eat. If the government finds out we're trying to build a village and farm this park land, it's gonna be hell to pay."

"George," said the young woman who had spoken first, putting her hand on his arm. "I know how you feel, believe me I do. But I don't think the government has a clue about what to do with us. And I for one don't want to spend the winter in a stinkin' tent with my kids when it's freezing and there's snow on the ground."

Liz stepped into the discussion. "Thank you, George, for being honest and right up front with your thoughts. I'm sure there are people here who agree with you. One of the ideas I'm trying to put forth is the importance of discussion, with everyone's viewpoint on the table. But I'm also promoting the idea that you vote on matters like this and the majority wins. So to the basic question, should we proceed with the idea of creating a village in this park that will provide permanent housing for you people? All in favor, hold up your hands."

Twelve hands went up.

"Those opposed?"

Two hands rose.

"What about you, sir?" Liz asked the man who did not vote.

"My group was undecided. Some liked the village idea, and about an equal number were quite skeptical about it."

"Thank you," Liz said. "Those agreeing to move ahead are in the majority, and we will do that." Looking at the man who did not vote, Liz said, "I hope as we work through this, your group will agree it's a good idea. And for those of you who voted no, I hope that won't prevent you from digging in along with those who support it to make this village idea work. It's only when we learn how to work together, even when we have differences, that we can do important things. And I can't think of anything more important right now than providing more permanent housing for all of you now living in tents."

That afternoon, Amos Charters, an Oldster and a retired engineer and surveyor, enlisted displaced persons to begin laying out the village, indicating with markers where the houses would be located. Once the location for each house was plotted, families would draw a number out of a hat, thereby choosing the spot for their new home.

Meanwhile, two Oldster former building contractors began showing the prospective homeowners how to build log cabin homes. Ample pine and maple trees were available in the park's hundred-acre woodlot, which was a part of the park. The contractors also found several cross-cut saws and axes that had been used when the place was known as Pioneer State Park and its staff offered demonstrations on log cabin building using these tools. The contractors visited the old water-powered sawmill located on the Crystal River, a short distance from the village that was quickly taking shape, and to their pleasant surprise, they discovered that with a little work it would once more operate.

Every day the new settlers—the name they preferred over refugees or displaced persons—could hear the ring of the ax and the yell, "timber," as yet another tree was felled. The park owner had offered hayrides to park visitors and the park owned two teams of Belgian work horses that pulled the wagons. Now the teams were used to snake the logs out of the woods, to the various building sites.

With considerable adjusting, repairing, and cleaning, the old sawmill was soon operational. Now the log cabin homes could have plank floors, furniture made of pine boards, and roofs with lumber and shingles sawed at the mill.

Spirits were high as late summer slipped into autumn. After a contest where people submitted names and then voted, the settlers chose New Start as the name for their village.

Meanwhile, Liz followed up with John Owens, who was beginning to organize a bartering system. He had noticed that people were already helping each other, trading basic goods, swapping a shirt for a hat, that sort of thing. But he knew there was potential for much more bartering to take place. His idea was to take bartering to a level where people were readily sharing their skills, talents, and possessions with each other.

John began creating a community skills inventory. He tacked a poster to the wall in the big community center building, with three headings:

Name
Skill or Goods to Offer
Payment Expected

Of course there was no circulating money, as everyone previously had to use Eagle credit cards for all their transactions. For the kind of work and activities the community was considering, John knew that they would have to abandon the Eagle credit cards and create a new system.

When people stopped by to sign up on the community skills list and asked about payment, John explained, "We are establishing a barter bank, which is based on two things: the nature of the skill offered and the number of hours involved. For instance, if your skill is teaching guitar playing, you might indicate two barter credits (BCs) for each hour of instruction, or if you indicate babysitting, you might indicate one BC per hour. You can in turn deposit your earned BCs in the barter bank. You withdraw BCs whenever you have the need for goods or services. You look at the list, find what you need, and then draw from the barter bank to make payment."

People quickly caught on to the system, which the barter bank managed. The bank was set up in one of the little offices connected to the park's community building and was operated by a volunteer who had skills in bookkeeping. In addition to keeping the records for each person's barter account, she helped connect people who needed something done with the skilled person who could do it. Within a few days, the barter bank became one of the busiest places in the village, as the settlers needed skills to help in everything from building a stone chimney for their cabin to learning how to snare a wild rabbit and prepare the meat over an open fire.

Andy, Liz, and Andy's brother, Herman, soon became the most popular bank customers as each day they brought a supply of fresh vegetables—cucumbers, carrots, cabbages, sweet corn, broccoli, and squash—to the community center, which they offered for barter credits, and which they promptly banked. As people lined up to "buy" the Schmidt produce, Andy talked to them about how next spring they could plant their own gardens and grow their own vegetables. And he would teach them how to do it.

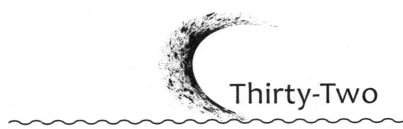

Thirty-Two

Pastor Larry was encouraged after talking with many of the settlers who had once been church members and who longed for a renewal of their spiritual lives. He had discovered that the settler group represented former Protestant and Catholic Church members as well as a few Jewish people, one or two Muslims, and several who had no church affiliation but knew the importance of a spiritual dimension in their lives.

On a cool Sunday morning, with the maple leaves beginning to color and the sky a vivid blue, Pastor Larry looked out over the couple hundred people who had jammed into the community room at the park headquarters building. All seats were filled and people were standing in the back and along the sides of the room. Earlier, Pastor Larry had posted signs throughout the village announcing that church services would be held at ten on Sunday mornings at the park headquarters.

Pastor Larry took the microphone and said, "I am so pleased to see you." He stopped for a moment and looked around the room. People continued to arrive and now were standing just outside the door.

"Thank you so much for coming. I hope that we can all be a blessing to each other, especially during this trying time in your lives." The room was quiet, without a sound from anyone as they listened to each word.

"I'm calling this gathering the Church of Hope. We have no special building, no book that we revere and believe to have all the answers, we have no liturgy, and we have no allegiance to some larger church group."

He stopped for a moment and brushed his hand across his forehead—the room was becoming warm.

"You are the Church of Hope. Each one of you alone and all of you together, this is your church."

The group responded with loud clapping, something that Pastor Larry had not expected.

He went on. "Not far from here, in a village called Link Lake, a group of church people not too different from you sought a new life in what were then the wilds of Wisconsin. They called themselves the Standalones, and they had the motto 'We stand alone as we stand together.' They knew the importance of each person, the value of each human life, but they also knew that individuality can only be expressed fully when we stand together, when we work together, play together, and yes, when we stand in front of God together."

Another round of applause erupted. It was something that Pastor Larry was not accustomed to hearing, but he was pleased to hear it because these once stranded and displaced individuals were learning the power of working together, of sharing talents and skills as they built their new homes and created a new community.

"The pastor for this ragtag group of settlers from New York State arrived here in Wisconsin with next to nothing," Pastor Larry continued. "They traveled by steamboat to Sheboygan, and then, with eight teams of oxen pulling eight wagons, they traveled west and founded the village of Link Lake.

"That pastor was Increase Joseph Link and he had a profound vision for his people and for this great state of Wisconsin, which has since become decimated by the antics of the politicians associated with the Eagle Party.

"I have the book that tells the story of Increase Joseph as his preaching became known first in central Wisconsin, and then throughout the state, and even beyond. I hid it away during the awful book burning that we all remember." He held up a tattered copy of *The Travels of Increase Joseph*.

"When the Standalone congregation gathered for its weekly meetings, they sang what became their standard hymn. I will try to sing it for you as I remember it."

Pastor Larry glanced around the overfilled and increasingly warm room. He took a handkerchief from his pocket, brushed it across his forehead, cleared his throat, and in a deep baritone voice began singing:

> We are alone together,
> Of God and the land
> Yet together we stand
> As alone we are too.
> Simple yet not
> A direction but no.
> We stand for the land
> May it always be so.

Pastor Larry continued. "I remember reading one of Preacher Increase Joseph's sermons. Here's what he said after he made one of his several trips to preach to ever larger crowds, and then returned to the Village of Link Lake to rest and recuperate. He had been disappointed in what he had observed people doing."

Pastor Larry opened the book, turned to a marked page, and began reading:

> The people are not listening.
> Their minds are clamped shut as tight as the lid on a pickle barrel.
> People are not listening to the land.
> You cannot know God without listening to the land.
> The land has a message for all of us, but we must learn to listen.
> We must hear its message and then heed it.
> We must capture in our minds what the land is telling us.
> People are driven by money. Money.
> They are listening to money and ignoring the land.
> Oh, the futility of their lives.
> What will it take to unstop their ears,
> To remove the blinders from their eyes?

Pastor Larry looked around the room. Not a sound. The group was listening, but he wondered, *Are they hearing and are they thinking? Do they realize that the reason they are here is because too many people did not listen to the land, did not listen to the natural world that surrounded them? They did not hear the message that became increasingly clear as they continued doing what they always did, trying to accumulate more and more wealth.*

He asked if anyone wished to come forward with either a prayer or a comment. Several people lined up and one by one took the microphone.

"I pray for my husband. I pray that he is still alive," said a young woman who burst into tears as she returned to her chair. The person sitting next to her gave her a big hug.

"We are blessed, truly blessed that we have found this place, this land where we can start our lives over. Truly blessed," an older woman said. Pastor Larry remembered the woman from the tent census he and Liz had done. She walked to the back of the room, her head held high.

A big, burly man slowly made his way to the front of the room. He took the microphone. "My name is Mike Carlson," he began, his voice filled with emotion. "I . . . I want to thank the McCabe family for taking in my wife, Jody, when she . . ." Carlson took out his handkerchief and blew his nose. He continued with a shaky voice. "When she became separated from the kids and me during the storm. It was so kind of them. They're sitting with my wife and kids in back of the room." A spontaneous round of applause erupted as Mike Carlson slowly made his way to his seat and everyone turned to see and cheer for this reunited family.

A man who had been sitting near the front of the room took the microphone.

"On behalf of all of us settlers, I want to extend my heartfelt thanks to the Oldsters. These people are volunteers. God sent these people to us, to help us, nurture us, and teach us. I, for one, feel that we are truly blessed to be in the midst of such wonderful people. Let's give Pastor Larry, Liz Carrall, and all the others who have been so generous on our behalf a big round of applause."

With those words, everyone jumped to their feet and applauded.

When Pastor Larry was able to capture the group's attention once more, he said, "Thank you so much, everyone. We'll see you all next week, and remember: When you listen to the land, you are listening to God."

Thirty-Three

The same day that Patrick O'Malley's summer job at the Crystal River Woodworks ended he received a message from Eagle University.

Because of extenuating circumstances, Eagle University has found it necessary to suspend all operations for the fall term. We will be in touch as soon as we are able to resume operation.

Director of Admissions, Eagle University

Patrick was very disappointed but he was not surprised. State and federal governmental operations had been strained to the breaking point as they tried to respond to the thousands of requests for aid and assistance coming from all parts of the country.

His parents were at work, so Patrick sat at the kitchen table, pondering what he should do. His mind went back to Onthaway and the training he had received. He knew that the Oldsters were volunteering at the park and wondered if he could help. He sent Liz Carrall a message.

Although she was disappointed when Patrick told her that Eagle University had temporarily closed its doors, she welcomed Patrick's offer to volunteer at New Start. She told him to stop by the headquarters building the following day so they could discuss what he might do to help the Oldsters with what became known as their "big idea."

When they met the next day, Liz told Patrick about the bartering system they had established with its barter credits and the barter bank. She mentioned that one of its problems was letting people know on a regular basis how many BCs they had banked.

"Oh, I think I can help you with this," Patrick said. "How about I work out a system where the barter bank can send each customer an encrypted message each month noting their BC balance on their SPEDs? Everyone still has one of those—right?" Patrick asked.

"Yes, they do. One of the good things we got from the government was these solar-powered devices. They continue to work just fine."

"I learned how to do encryption at Onthaway Academy," Patrick said. "This Canadian guy who taught us really knew his stuff. And I've been practicing ever since—without the OSR ever finding out," he said proudly.

Liz was thinking ahead, answering in her mind a question that she had been wondering about: how to inform the various Oldster chapters operating in the Midwest what her group was doing at the village of New Start and encourage other Oldsters to do something similar.

"Patrick," she said, feeling excited. "Would you know how to send an encrypted newsletter to all the Oldster groups in the Midwest? I have their SPED addresses—got them when we were still working at Onthaway Academy."

"Sure, nothing to it," Patrick said. "It'd work the same way as sending barter bank BC information. I'd send the newsletter encrypted so the OSR couldn't snoop."

"Wonderful," said Liz. "Thank you, Patrick. Thank you. Let's have you get started on this right away." She gave him a big hug and he blushed.

"I learned something else at Onthaway," Patrick said quietly. "I learned the rudiments of how to hack. I've kept in touch with the Canadian fellow who is helping me learn more, and I've gotten quite good at hacking, if I must say so myself."

"You learned what?"

"I learned how to get inside other people's computer systems. I've been reading the local OSR messages for the past several weeks. They believe your Oldster chapter is just the best. The regional OSR says the same thing. I'll bet you didn't know that the regional office plans on giving your group what they call their 'coveted public service award.'"

"Well, I'll be," said Liz, more than surprised by the information. "If they only knew what we were really trying to do."

"I also learned," said Patrick, "that the OSR office plans to begin flying their drones again on a limited basis. Since the big storm, they've had them all grounded."

"Well, we haven't seen one around here. Good thing—one of those drones with a camera and a listening device might pick up some information we surely wouldn't want them to know. They might even cancel our special award," Liz said, laughing.

"Well, don't tell anyone," Patrick said in a near whisper, "but I've figured out how to hack into the controls for a particular drone and fly it where I want it to go. I tried it just the other day when the OSR sent up a drone. I let them fly it around Crystal River for a few minutes, then I took control of it and flew it before turning it back to their controllers. They didn't even know they'd been hacked. I read one of their messages—it said, *Lost control of one of our drones today. Must be solar interference.* They didn't have a clue about what really happened."

"Patrick, I've got to get you in touch with Joe Vogel," Liz said. "He's in charge of security at New Start. He could surely use your help, especially with the threat of drones returning."

Part VII

October

Thirty-Four

Following her vision that lifelong learning was an essential part of society, Liz began organizing what she called "Learn-Ins." Some of the workshops lasted one or two sessions, while others carried on for several weeks.

She had in mind three types of Learn-Ins. One type would focus on the big questions of how to organize a community. Another would focus on smaller practical matters such as how to plant a garden, make furniture, treat injuries and illnesses, and similar topics. The third would cover creative and recreational pursuits, such as writing, painting, and learning how to play an instrument.

Liz's first Learn-In would be held on three successive Wednesday mornings. She called it "From There to Here: Making a Community." She was surprised when fifty people showed up for the first session and pleased that these refugees were eager to make their newly formed village work.

She decided to conduct the workshop much as she had done at Onthaway Academy. She asked how many people had with them their copy of *A Guide for a Moral Society*. Most people had them and Liz had a few extras for those who didn't. As she had done at Onthaway, she asked the attendees to divide into smaller groups of six to eight each, and asked that each select one person as a recorder-spokesperson. Then Liz said, "Here's what I want you to do. Look at the *Guide for a Moral Society* and discuss the assumptions that are behind each of the guidelines."

"Whoa," said an older fellow sitting in the front row. "What do you mean 'discuss assumptions'? Isn't the *Guide* a revered book, like the Holy Bible that many of us remember before the Eagle Power took power and got rid of the churches? And what is an assumption, anyway?"

"Okay, let me start with your last question. What is an assumption? Try this: What were the people who wrote the *Guide* thinking when they wrote this book? What did they think was most important for a society? And as for your first question, well you'll have to decide for yourself if you have the right to critically examine the *Guide*. But let me offer my opinion—and maybe you'll think this is extreme—but the very reason that you are here, that your beloved Door County has been devastated, is because of this book."

A gasp went up from the audience. Apparently the refugees had not made the connection that the book that they were supposed to carry with them at all times had anything to do with the challenges they faced. She flipped over a page of newsprint clipped to an easel to reveal the guidelines listed in *A Guide for a Moral Society*:

> Success is measured by wealth.
> Avoid joining groups—they sap the energy from individual
> achievement.
> If you are not a winner, you are a loser.
> Avoid thinking; it gets in the way of productivity.
> Never question authority; respect it.
> Hard workers do not need excuses.
> The greatest friend you have is yourself.
> Winning is everything.
> Immigration should be stopped.
> The environment and its resources are there for our use.

"See that last statement," Liz said. "The one about the environment. The Eagle Party has a very narrow view, believing that the environment is something that is just there, and that human beings have little influence over it. The Eagle Party has ignored the scientific evidence about climate change that was available when they took office. Scientists had quite accurately predicted what would happen if steps weren't taken to slow down global warming and its effects. The Eagle Party not only ignored it, but they refused to allow any more research to take place, and they prevented people from talking about it. After the Eagle Party took over, university scientists were prevented from doing any further work on the topic."

Liz pointed to the statements from *A Guide for a Moral Society.* "Any more questions?"

The small groups quickly formed and the discussion was lively—and sometimes heated. Liz walked around the room, listening in on some of the conversations. "Wow," she heard a young woman say. "We never did anything like this in school. This is kind of fun." An older person commented, "We're looking at the future. It may be fun, but it's also pretty serious stuff. I wonder what would happen if the OSR people could see what we're doing?"

In another group, members were stuck on the statement "If you are not a winner, you are a loser." An older woman asked, "So what else is there if there aren't just winners and losers?"

"Why do we have to put people in one or the other category? Why can't people just be—just be people?" asked a young man. He seemed to be thinking very deeply about the assumptions behind the statement.

The following Wednesday, everyone from the first workshop attended, plus several more. And once more the discussion was sometimes heated, but never boring. At the third session, Liz asked the participants to design what she called a set of rules, rights, and responsibilities for the new village of New Start and the citizens who lived there. The group selected six people who called themselves the Triple R Group to develop this new document, and that smaller committee met several times before its members agreed the draft of Rules, Rights, and Responsibilities was ready to be put to a vote by all the citizens of New Start.

Liz was pleased with the progress the community was making toward deciding what they wanted to become. They were clearly on their way to becoming self-sufficient and a model community whose efforts Liz could share with other Oldster groups.

In the fall, the citizens of New Start elected their first mayor. There had been a brisk campaign between two candidates. With an earlier recommendation from the Triple R Group, a majority of New Start citizens agreed that everyone sixteen years old and older should have the right to vote. The turnout for the election was close to 100 percent. At that time the citizens also elected a three-person court whose responsibility would be to resolve any disputes among the citizens. Finally, they voted on a Statement of Rules, Rights, and Responsibilities that had its beginning in Liz's community-building Learn-In.

The statement included:

> Everyone has the right to be treated equally.
>
> People should have the freedom to think and believe as they wish.
>
> Everyone should care for others as they wish others to care for them.
>
> While individuality is respected, cooperation with others is essential.
>
> Each person's creativity is respected and its expression encouraged.
>
> The arts, such as music, creative writing, painting, and dance, are a fundamental part of the community.
>
> Every person aged sixteen and older has the right to participate in the decision-making of the group.
>
> Cooperation is encouraged over competition.
>
> Personal value is not measured by the accumulation of wealth and material possessions.
>
> There will be universal respect for and every effort made to protect the environment: the water and the air, the land and all that lives on it and in it.
>
> Opportunities for lifelong learning will be abundant.
>
> Each person has the responsibility to abide by these rules, and when there is dispute, a panel of three judges will act.

Thirty-Five

Sully Sorenson came from New York City in his own jet. He came with an idea and with little knowledge about what had happened at Happy Valley Park, which he had purchased almost ten years ago from the Eagle Party. He had seen the park as an investment, a chance to make some easy money since the government sold the park at a rock-bottom price—compared to New York City real estate investments, anyway.

He had been irate when the federal government declared an emergency after the Door County catastrophe. The government had said they would pay the park owners a "reasonable rent" until the refugees could be removed from the park. But so far, Sorenson had gotten no rent payment and no word about when the refugees would leave his park.

The driver approached the entrance to the park, opened the window of the black limousine, and spoke with the sentry at the gate, who on this day happened to be Joe Vogel.

"What is the nature of your business?" Joe asked, leaning down for a look inside the expensive car. He couldn't remember the last time he had seen a limo.

"My boss just wants to visit, to look around," the driver said.

"What's his name?" asked Vogel.

"It's Sorenson, Sully Sorenson. We've traveled all the way from New York City, so please stand aside so we can enter."

When Joe Vogel heard the name, his face turned white and he had to catch his breath. He gathered back his poise and said, "Could I speak with Mr. Sorenson, please?"

Joe saw the driver turn his head, push back the little window separating the driver's compartment from the passenger section, and say something to his boss sitting in back. A tall, thin man with closely cropped gray hair, wearing a black suit and a purple shirt with no tie, stepped from the limo and approached Joe, whose hands were shaking.

Sorenson extended his hand to a bearded Joe Vogel and said, "Name is Sully Sorenson and I own this park." He looked carefully at Joe, stood back, and said, "Don't I know you? You . . . you're Joe Stewart."

"You must have me confused with someone else," said Joe. "My name's Joe Vogel."

"Come on now, Joe, this is your old buddy Sully. You haven't forgotten all those miserable months we spent together in Afghanistan—too many years ago? What's with the beard? You always said you'd never wear one."

"Keep your voice down, Sully. Everyone here knows me as Joe Vogel."

"What in hell are you doing here, in the middle of nowhere? Last I heard you were working for the federal OSR."

"I was, until I got an assignment up here to check out this local group."

"So are you still working for the OSR?"

"Nope, I decided I was done with all that. I met these remarkable people up here. They call themselves Oldsters. I help with their volunteer work."

"Well, what do you know?" Sully said, seeming amused at seeing the hard-boiled Joe Stewart in his new role as a retired volunteer. He remembered Joe as a trained "never-miss" sniper with more kills to his credit that any of the other snipers working at the time.

"So what brings you here?" asked Joe, trying not to show his nervousness.

"I own this park," said Sorenson. "I bought it when the state sold all the parks. I thought something here in the Midwest would be a good investment. The state said I'd get it back as soon as the refugees left. Are they gone?"

Joe thought fast. He could tell Sorenson that the refugees had left or were packing up to go in hopes that he would climb back into his limo, leave, and forget that he had ever seen Joe Stewart. That was his best hope so that no one at the OSR would find out he had managed to fake his own death. But it wouldn't take much for Sorenson to find out he was lying. For just a moment he thought, *My life's been a lie ever since I became Joe Vogel and moved here. What's one more lie?* But then he decided it was time he began telling the truth.

"No, they haven't left, and they don't plan on leaving," he said. "They've built new homes here and have created their own community. They call their village New Start. I can show it to you, if you'd like."

"Jesus, Joe, are you telling me that these people took over my land without a thought that someone else might own it?"

"That's about it," said Joe.

"Well, that's not right. I'll get in touch with the militia. I've got financial means, Joe, and you know better than most that wealth means power."

Joe stood silently, watching Sorenson weigh the situation. Then Sully said, "I've never made much off this investment. It was a big mistake to buy it. But I've got a plan for turning that around. Do these people have any funds? Can they pay me for the land?"

"Sully, they've got nothing," Joe told him. "They were forced out of their homes when the weather companies didn't give them enough warning before a big storm hit Door County. Most of them barely had clothes on their backs when they showed up here."

"That's not my problem," Sorenson said gruffly. "Are you gonna give me a tour, let me see for myself what's going on here—what these people are doing with my property?"

"Sure, I'll give you a tour, if you promise to keep your mouth shut about who I really am. And don't shoot off your mouth to these people about how you really own this place and hope they'll leave here as soon as possible. You'd better park the limo down the road a bit, out of sight. People see that thing and they'll start asking questions. I'll drive you around in my car."

With the limo parked, Sully climbed into Joe's car and they drove around the park, past the new log cabins and along the fields, where men were driving horses and plowing the land where they planned to plant winter wheat before the ground froze. Sully said nothing, shaking his head occasionally in disbelief.

More than a mile from the emerging village, where the road had become a two-lane trail, Sully said, "Stop here. I want to show you something."

Both men got out of the car. Sully explained, "My guess is you don't know this is here. I stumbled on it by accident when I looked around before buying this place."

Joe, ever cautious, wondered if this was a ploy for Sully to hike him out into the dense woods and kill him. What if the OSR knew Bill hadn't eliminated him after all? And what if Sully was a secret OSR agent? He made sure that Sully walked ahead of him, along the faint trail. Joe remembered that Sully was known for his tracking ability. He could find a trail that was invisible to most people. Joe began to perspire as they hiked along.

"There it is," said Sully. "Look down there, Joe."

Joe looked to where he was pointing. He saw water bubbling out of the ground and a little stream running toward the Crystal River in the valley below.

"That, my friend, is a spring," said Sully. "And that spring is gonna make me even richer than I am now."

"What are you thinking?" said Joe, confused.

"I'm going to build a bottling plant right here where we are standing. I'm going to call the water 'Crystal River Best: The Purest Water in the World.'" He smiled broadly.

"But what about the settlers? They're no more than a mile away."

"To hell with the settlers. They can have their sorry little village and they can farm away with their horses and plows. My bottling plant will make me millions. Pure water is not easy to come by anymore. And we both know that this water is pure."

This was a point on which Joe and Sully could agree.

"Tell you what, Joe Stewart-Vogel, you keep your mouth shut about my plans and make sure that nobody gets in my way when we start building our bottling plant and I won't tell anybody who you really are, and what you are really good at doing. I don't think this bunch of primitive settlers would like to hear that they have a trained assassin in their midst."

Was this something he could accept? The thought that raced through his mind was: *What choice do I have? I have too much to lose.*

"Agreed," said Joe, quietly.

A week later, Liz Carall spoke to Joe as he was poring over the sentry volunteer schedule for the coming week.

"Say, Joe, what's going on over in the back corner of the park? Sounds like some big machines working."

Joe tried to compose himself so his response would sound natural. "I checked it out, Liz. Someone's building something outside the park, not far from the river. Don't know what it is, but it should be of no concern to the New Start folks," he lied. "I'll keep an eye on the operation myself, to make sure the construction work doesn't harm the park in any way."

Joe felt awful about lying to Liz. He trusted her, respected her leadership, and was impressed with the vision she had for this group and for the country. *But what can I do?* he thought. Sorenson had him over a barrel. If he told anyone what was happening inside the park, near the spring that had been free flowing since the last glacier receded ten thousand years ago, his cover would be blown. *If these good people find out about my past, I don't know what they'll do to me. And there's still the possibility that the OSR will somehow discover that I am still alive, and send someone to silence me once and for all.*

Thirty-Six

Patrick O'Malley and Joe Vogel met several times to discuss how Patrick's computer skills could help protect New Start from drone visits. Joe was most impressed with Patrick's ability to hack into and fly a drone without the pilot realizing that he or she had been hacked.

Patrick and Joe were chatting about this one afternoon at the entrance gate to New Start when they both heard the unmistakable hum of a drone. Immediately, Patrick took out his SPED, quickly moved his fingers over the screen, and, smiling, said, "Got it." They watched the drone approaching.

Joe watched Patrick use his customized SPED to turn the machine, slow it, and land it right at their feet. "Amazing," said Joe. "Absolutely amazing." A little blue light on the drone continued to blink on and off as the rotors continued spinning. Patrick poked his SPED screen a few more times, and the blue light went out and the rotors stopped spinning.

"Looks like we got ourselves a drone," said Patrick. "I'm sure we can find uses for it here, wouldn't you say, Joe?"

"I'm sure we can," Joe agreed, shaking his head in disbelief at what he had just observed.

Patrick picked up the drone. He noticed that it had a sophisticated video camera, along with a long-reach microphone. Patrick was thinking ahead. He could use the video camera to record happenings at New Start and include them with the *New Start News* that was now transmitting weekly to all the Oldster chapters active in the upper Midwest, thanks to Liz's SPED address list.

"Won't the OSR people come looking for their missing drone?" Joe asked. "Those things have to be expensive."

"I don't think so," Patrick said. "I hacked into their communication system last week, and one of their drones apparently got caught in a solar flare. They lost communication and never found the drone. Apparently solar flares are causing lots of problems with drones now. They'll probably think that caused them to lose another one."

Patrick carried the drone to the headquarters building, where he found Liz working in her little office.

"Hey, what have you got there, Patrick?" she asked excitedly as he walked in.

"Got myself a drone," he answered, smiling from ear to ear. "Newest model, too. It's got a fancy solar-powered digital video camera and a high-powered microphone to even pick up conversations within a building. It was headed our way and I captured it just in time."

As Liz was admiring the drone, Patrick continued. "What I'm thinking is that I'd like to see if we can use the video camera to record some of the goings-on here, and then include the video material within our regular edition of the *New Start News.*"

"Excellent idea, Patrick. Thank you. This will really help any Oldster group that's skeptical about what we're trying to do here so they can see for themselves what's going on. Let's just be sure to inform the citizens of New Start, so they understand this drone works for the good guys."

"Also, I've been working with a young lady from Door County who is quite interested in all of this stuff. She's also a good writer. I'm thinking we might be able to turn the *New Start News* over to her, and whomever else she might select to help."

"That's another good idea," said Liz. "One of our goals is to make this community entirely self-supporting, with only minimal help from us. Putting them in charge of their own electronic newspaper is surely one way of getting there."

Before year's end, an enhanced and encrypted *New Start News* was received weekly by Oldster chapters throughout the Midwest, as well as by several new chapters that had recently organized in New England. The states along the Atlantic Coast, where flooding continued to inundate low-lying communities, had been especially successful in launching Oldster chapters. Marilyn Barnes, the new editor of the *News*, and her staff of five reporters plus two videographers had been busy interviewing people in New Start and writing stories about their activities, from the various Learn-In workshops to the results of the recently held elections.

Marilyn invited other Oldster groups to send in their success stories as well. She was especially interested in the innovative ways they were able to baffle their local OSR offices while continuing to carry out their task of encouraging a social revolution in the country. With help from Liz Carall, the electronic newspaper carried stories about the various workshops once offered at the now-closed Onthaway Academy. Liz was hopeful that perhaps if enough Oldsters were interested, a new Onthaway Academy would open—perhaps right here in the village of New Start.

The Crystal River Oldsters received a letter of commendation from regional OSR director Tracy Smith, recognizing them for their "outstanding volunteer efforts in helping meet a crisis of epic proportions." A few weeks later, Liz learned from one of Patrick's hacked OSR messages that Tracy had returned to her home state of Ohio after receiving a promotion for the good work she had done as regional director in Wisconsin. Liz thought, *If those folks in Ohio knew what the Crystal River Oldsters had really been doing right under Tracy's nose, she would probably be in jail, or even eliminated.*

Noting the continued success of the *New Start News*, Patrick stopped by to see Liz as she was winding up a morning Learn-In workshop.

"Got another idea," he said when he sat down across from Liz, who had just poured herself a cup of coffee.

"You are just full of ideas," Liz said, patting the young man on the arm.

"I've found a way to hack into the electronic mailing list for the *National Eagle Reporter*. What if we sent a weekly message embedded in the *Reporter* that several million people receive on their SPEDs? We could call it something like "Creating a New Society." We could include information about what is happening here at New Start, without being specific about our location so nobody could find us. What do you think?"

"Excellent idea, Patrick. Excellent. Let's talk with Emily Taylor. She's a former English teacher and writing instructor. This sounds like another great project for our Oldsters."

Part VIII

September,
One Year Later

Thirty-Seven

Liz Carall looked at John Owens, who said, "The listening device is disabled, but frankly it doesn't even look like it functions anymore. It's so dusty I doubt it would pick up much even if it was hooked up."

"Thank you, John," Liz said. "I haven't seen a drone in the past three months. They must still have big budget problems."

"Brought that on themselves," he said.

"Well, welcome back, everyone. I trust you've all had a good summer. Let's start with some reports. Emily, how are memorabilia sales?"

"Not good. Nothing like they were before the Door County catastrophe. There are fewer visitors these days, and they aren't nearly as interested in wearing an Eagle Party cap or buying an Eagle Party sweatshirt."

"Andy, what about the Crystal River flower project?"

"It's doing okay. We've had a very hot summer, as you know. I've got to consider some different flower varieties for next summer. Every summer seems a little hotter than the previous one."

"I know you all want a report on happenings at New Start," said Liz. "Let's start with you, Joe. As you all know, Joe Vogel has been training the volunteer security force at the village."

"Got a good group of volunteers," Joe began. "Really, there's so little going on that about all they need to do is station one person at the gate to check out any visitors, and assign a couple people to patrol the village streets at night to keep any mischief in check. But there've been almost no problems. People seem very happy to have their own homes. They take good care of them, and they help each other spot any trouble before it happens."

"Pleased to hear it," Liz said.

"Back to you, Andy. How about the farming operations at New Start?"

"Excellent. As most of you know, I've held Learn-Ins where we talked about everything from preventing soil erosion to how to grow crops such as wheat for flour and sweet sorghum to use in place of sugar. By the way, the winter wheat crop was outstanding. And with the help of the engineers in this group"—Andy pointed to the two Oldster engineers—"we were able to not only keep the water-powered sawmill operating but also divert some of the waterpower to the old flour mill that once again is grinding wheat into flour. Folks will have plenty of flour this winter. One problem, though—for some reason, each month the Crystal River seems to be lower and flowing more slowly. This is a real problem, one we'll need to do something about. Clean, fresh water is essential to the lives of everyone in New Start, and we need a good stream flow to operate the sawmill and the flour mill."

Joe Vogel cringed when he heard this. He knew the reason for the river's decreased flow—the bottled water plant that he allowed to operate in the far corner of the park. Joe had encouraged his old army buddy, and now blackmailer, Sully Sorenson to fence off the bottling plant operation to make it look like it was not within the park boundaries. Sorenson had guards patrolling the bottling plant twenty-four hours a day to keep people away. The trucks that hauled away the bottled water were entirely enclosed and were marked with the words "Sorenson's Sand and Gravel" to disguise what they were really hauling.

Andy continued with his report. "I held six garden Learn-Ins, each well attended. With the warm weather and rains we've had this past growing season, the gardens have been outstanding. Everyone has plenty of fresh vegetables to eat this summer, and a couple of the settlers who know how to preserve vegetables demonstrated how to dry and can vegetables and make sauerkraut out of cabbage."

"Thank you, Andy." Liz smiled at her husband. Andy had been her major supporter when she felt miserable, especially when so many of her early ideas for creating a social revolution had sputtered along, or failed.

"I declare New Start a success," Liz said proudly. "Thanks to each of you who volunteered your services and risked being punished severely if the OSR found out what we were really doing." Everyone clapped. "The village and its occupants are moving toward self-sufficiency. The barter bank is working. People are readily sharing their skills and knowledge with each other and accumulating and spending their barter credits. As Andy has pointed out, they are farming and gardening together and readily sharing what they are harvesting, and they are learning the importance of taking care of the environment. They are also learning how to cooperate, although it will take a while for them to move past the idea that the only way to make it in the world is to compete. And they are having fun. I attended the barn dance the other night—some of you were there—and they were all dancing and laughing and having a great time. They've put together their own little village band—I don't know where they found the instru-ments, must have bartered for them, but just three guys, one with a banjo, one with a violin, and one playing a button concertina were making great music together."

Liz stopped for a moment and looked down at her notes. She continued. "Before I forget, I want to especially thank Patrick O'Malley for all that he has done to help our cause. You all know that Patrick won a scholarship to attend Eagle University in Marshfield last year. Since the university closed, Patrick has been helping us. Patrick, come up here."

A bashful and reluctant Patrick O'Malley walked to where Liz was speaking.

"Patrick," Liz began. "You have been an excellent Oldster Associate. I know you are a long way from being sixty years old, but we have voted to suspend our age rule in your case and make you a full-fledged member of the Crystal River Oldsters."

Everyone jumped to their feet and clapped as Patrick, more than a little embarrassed by all the attention, blushed. Liz gave him a big hug.

While Patrick stood next to her, staring at his shoelaces, Liz began reciting the litany of contributions that he had made to the group. "First, let me say that Patrick is a computer whiz. We all carry around these

SPEDs and read the messages that the Eagle Party wants us to read. But some of you know that Patrick, thanks to his training at the Onthaway Academy and his follow-up work, not only knows how to encrypt messages so we can easily communicate with other Oldster chapters, but he also set up an encryption system that allows the barter bank to keep in touch with its customers. But that's not all. Patrick knows how to get into the OSR message system without their knowing it. Now, with Patrick's help, we can keep track of what they are doing. But best of all, Patrick has figured out a way to place stories of social change that's occurring around the country in the digital *National Eagle Reporter*, which everyone receives every day. It's driving the national office crazy because Patrick is able to make it look like the stories are coming from different parts of the country, when they are really coming from right here in Crystal River, Wisconsin."

Liz stopped speaking again and motioned toward Patrick, who was pulling at one ear and running his hand through his hair, and looking more and more uncomfortable with all the attention he was getting. "Let's give Patrick one more round of applause."

Patrick smiled broadly as he returned to his chair, and those seated next to him patted him on the back.

"And one final thing," Liz continued. "I've heard from several Oldster Groups, especially those that remember Onthaway Academy. They are encouraging us to start another such training program right here. What do you think? Dare we open what we could call an Onthaway Learning Center at New Start? Think about it."

Just in case the OSR might by some remote chance be listening in, John enabled the listening device, nodded to Liz, and the group began singing songs that they remembered from when they were growing up: "I've Got My Love to Keep Me Warm," "Harbor Lights," and ending with the "Beer Barrel Polka."

Thirty-Eight

On a warm and rather humid September morning, Liz and Andy Schmidt enjoyed a second cup of coffee as they looked over their field of garden crops. They had been harvesting since June and continued to do so nearly every day. Their garden stand in Crystal River provided them with a steady income of both Eagle credits they received from visitors and citizens of Crystal River and barter credits from their neighbors in New Start.

"Well, Liz," Andy said, breaking the silence. "I think it's working."

"What's working?" Liz answered, thinking he was referring to their garden.

"What the Oldster groups are doing around the country."

"Seems so," said Liz, "but we've sure had our ups and downs."

"Yes, we have, but hearing about the People's Party emerging over in Minnesota gives us hope that maybe people will realize what the Eagle Party has been doing to them and vote them out," said Andy. "And there is no doubt about it; the experiment with New Start is more than I ever expected. Those folks are happy and doing well."

"Yes, they certainly are. And I just heard from an Oldster chapter in North Dakota that they are working with a little rural community that had just disappeared when their oil wells dried up. The North Dakota chapter is using New Start as a model. And so far, the OSR has left them alone," Liz said, smiling.

"Well, I've got to get myself organized," she went on. "We're starting our first group of Oldster reps at the Onthaway Learning Center today. Andy, do you know that we've now got Oldster chapters in twenty states? And Patrick O'Malley and some of his buddies around the country have figured out a way to sneak through the OSR barriers and help Oldsters keep in touch with each other. We've got the Oldster chapters sending encrypted messages to each other. They're all talking about how a new society might look and getting people to believe that it might work. And I'm hoping that our new version of Onthaway Academy will help move things along."

After Liz pulled on her hiking shoes, shouldered her backpack, and left for her mile walk to New Start, Andy headed for the garden. It was time to cut some cabbage heads and make a batch of sauerkraut. As he walked toward a small cabbage patch, he noticed a bank of clouds building in the west. Andy couldn't afford to pay for the weather reports that the local for-profit weather company provided, and besides, since the Door County catastrophe, no one trusted the weather reports anyway. He thought to himself, *Could use a good rain—late-maturing garden stuff will be even better with a good soaking.*

Andy worked that morning, gathering up plump cabbage heads and then carrying them to the kitchen, where he used the same cabbage slicer that his mother used to make sauerkraut so many years ago. He worked carefully, recalling his mother's words: "Be careful, Andy, that cabbage slicer will snip off the end of a finger as fast it can slice a head of cabbage."

He washed out the old six-gallon Red Wing crock, the same one his mother had used. He began dumping shredded cabbage into the crock, covering each layer with salt, and packing it down with the same wooden stick his mother had used. The morning flew by. He enjoyed the smell of fresh cabbage, and his mind wandered back to when he was a kid and his family ate sauerkraut several times a week: baked sauerkraut, fried sauerkraut, sauerkraut and ham, and even sauerkraut cake that this mother baked in their wood-burning stove oven.

When he finished making sauerkraut, he ate a quick lunch and took a half-hour nap. He woke up to the growl of thunder in the distance. As he put on his hat and headed back to the garden, he saw the dark clouds now much closer. A jagged flash of lightning cut across the clouds that tumbled and turned on each other. And then came a much louder clap of thunder.

Liz and Emily heard the thunder, too. They were working with a group of twenty Oldsters from as many states, teaching them how their Oldster chapters could help with the social revolution that they all had come to believe was necessary. Emily began shutting windows in the community room. She glanced out the window to the west and saw the storm clouds moving in their direction. *It's been a hot, rainy summer*, she thought. *And here comes another storm.*

Patrick O' Malley saw the flash of lightning and heard the thunder as well. He had volunteered to help Marilyn Barnes, editor of the *New Start News*, do a story on the Crystal River's decreasing flow by shooting some video along the river where it threaded through the park.

Joe Vogel had come to the park with Emily, and while she was busy working with Liz and the Oldsters in the newly formed Onthaway Learning Center, he decided to take a walk along the river. His mind was a jumble of thoughts these days. He was well aware that the water bottling plant was the primary reason why the river's flow had diminished by half over the past several months. But he also knew that his life was in grave danger if the OSR learned he was still alive. He was sure Sully Sorenson would let the world know that Joe Vogel was really Joe Stewart, a former hired killer for the Office for Social Responsibility. His thoughts were interrupted when he saw the flash of lightning and heard the rumble of thunder. Then Joe spotted Patrick taking video of the slow-moving stream.

"Hey there, Joe," Patrick said when he saw his friend approaching. "What're you doing out here?"

"Just taking a little walk. From the look of those clouds we're both gonna get wet," answered Joe.

As the first raindrops began to fall, Joe and Patrick huddled under a big black oak tree that was a few yards from the river. Its thick canopy of leaves would keep them mostly dry as they waited for the shower to pass. Neither of them had seen the black twisting-and-turning funnel cloud that roared directly toward them. It was only a few yards wide, but its menacing, rotating wind tore lose everything in its path, lifting what it could high in the air to be dropped miles away.

"What's that noise?" asked Patrick. "I've never heard a sound like that."

"It's a tornado," yelled Joe over the sound of the killer twister. Now it was only a few yards from where they huddled under the big oak.

"Get down! Get down!" yelled Joe as he pushed Patrick to the ground and covered the young man with his own body as the sound of oak wood breaking and splintering filled the air.

Thirty-Nine

Andy watched the storm from his back porch. He saw the tornado cloud touch down ever so briefly and then lift back up into the sky like an angry fist retreating into a glove. He was sure the tornado had touched down in the vicinity of New Start, and he immediately thought of Liz. He took his SPED from his pocket and sent a message: "Are you OK?"

He waited a minute or two, but there was no reply. Rain was falling in torrents, more rain than he had ever seen fall so quickly in his lifetime. The ditches along the country road that trailed past his farm were filled with water that was running toward the river, dirty brown water that was gushing from his vegetable garden.

He grabbed his tattered raincoat and ran along the now muddy road toward the park. He was worried that Liz might be caught in the storm. As he hurried toward the village, Andy could see that the Crystal River, docile and slow moving for days, was now a raging torrent, tearing over its banks, destroying everything in its path. He made it over the little wooden bridge just before it collapsed. He saw pieces of the bridge's supports tumbling over and over and then disappearing from sight in the muddy raging torrent. He reached the headquarters building, out of breath, to find Liz, Emily, and the twenty out-of-town Oldsters watching the deluge.

With the tornado now several miles away and their SPEDs once more working, they heard, "Help, Help! It's Joe. Joe's hurt. Joe's hurt bad. We're on the hill by the river. Come quick. Joe's hurt bad."

"Oh no," cried Emily as she burst into tears. "Oh no, not my Joe."

Andy, upon hearing Patrick's cry for help, immediately ran into the falling rain. He could scarcely see a dozen feet in front of him as he ran through the storm, yelling into his SPED, "We're coming, Patrick. We're coming." Emily and Liz followed close behind.

"They're here," yelled Andy. "Right up ahead. I see them."

He ran to the pair on the ground. "What's wrong?" asked Andy as the driving rain pelted him in the face.

"It's Joe," sobbed Patrick. "He's hurt. He's bleeding."

Patrick had torn off his shirt and was holding it against a gaping hole in Joe's back, where blood was turning the cloth a crimson red. Patrick pointed to the three-foot-long splinter of oak wood, its sharp end red with blood.

"That branch speared Joe in the back," cried Patrick. "He, he was on top of me, shielding me from the storm. Joe . . . Joe saved my life."

A moment later, Emily and Liz arrived at the horrific scene. "What's wrong with Joe? Is he hurt? Oh, God, he's bleeding." Emily now focused on Patrick holding the blood-soaked shirt on Joe's wound. She kneeled down and bent over Joe, who was still conscious.

"Oh, Joe, Joe. I'm so sorry, so sorry," she said, her tears mixing with the rain that continued falling in torrents. A trickle of red-stained rainwater slowly flowed away from the tragic scene.

"Emily," whispered a dying Joe Vogel. "I . . . I love you." He paused, trying to muster the little strength he had left. "Thank you for . . ." His head fell back; his mouth was open but there were no more words.

Emily fell across the prone body of her friend and lover, her body racked with grief.

It wasn't until early evening that the group of Oldsters who had been working at New Start learned the full extent of the storm. The rain had stopped, but the Crystal River continued to flow over its banks. Within minutes it had flooded much of the Town of Crystal River, including all the homes and businesses near the river.

By early evening, those who had been flooded out of their homes were lined up at the entrance to New Start seeking a place to spend the night and stay dry until the floodwaters receded and they could return home. When Patrick saw his parents, he ran to them and they hugged one another. "Are you okay?" Patrick asked them.

"Just a little wet," said Patrick's father. "Just a little wet."

Upon seeing the long line of people at the entrance to their village, residents of New Start quickly began building a temporary bridge across the roaring Crystal River so they could welcome them in their high and dry village that looked down on the wild river. They knew too well what it was like to have a home flooded.

September, One Year Later

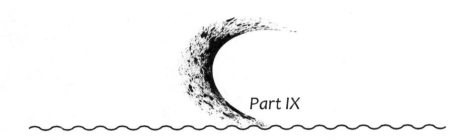

Part IX

Five Years Later

Forty

In the most recent US presidential election, the People's Party candidate, Olaf Norsman from Minnesota, handily bested the Eagle Party incumbent president, John Emery. Norsman's election brought with him enough Senate and House of Representative candidates from the People's Party to give him a majority in both houses. Thirty states, including Wisconsin, ousted their Eagle Party governors. The Oldster organization, now with Oldster chapters in every state of the nation, took some of the credit for the political tsunami that had swept the country. But the feeble response of the previous government's administration to the disasters that befell both coasts had much to do with the election results. In addition to the catastrophe in Door County, elsewhere thousands of homes and businesses had been destroyed and out-of-control fires had raged in the Northwest. The majority of the people now knew that the disastrous effects of climate change were real—many of them because they had experienced it personally.

The Eagle Party had promised to keep people safe. But in their zeal to protect borders and keep out immigrants, the Party had failed to recognize the enemy that was in their midst—climate change. And because the subject of climate change was prohibited from being taught in any of the schools, indeed could not even be mentioned, few people knew about its challenges.

In his first hundred days in office, President Norsman established a cabinet-level Department for Climate Change and Environmental Protection (DCCEP). It employed the best climate scientists in the country—many of whom had been secretly researching strategies for slowing down global warming that was occurring, as well as developing approaches for adjusting to the changes that were taking place as a result of a warmer world. The president immediately sent a delegation to attend an emergency climate change conference in Stockholm. A major unit in the DCCEP focused on water, as ensuring sufficient clean water for human consumption and for growing crops was already a challenge in the United States and around the globe.

With the support of Congress, President Norsman made available generous federal funding to the country's research universities, which quickly geared up research programs that they had been prohibited from doing, including climate change research and studies related to water quality, pollution detection in aquifers, and equitable fresh water distribution systems. A central theme of this research focused on the relationship between the environment and society. A subtheme examined the use of pesticides and herbicides on plants and the adverse effects on people from eating vegetables and fruit that had been treated with them. Research programs especially examined the negative results babies experienced when they were fed rice cereal that was grown on soil laced with inorganic arsenic. The use of antibiotics to encourage the growth of beef, hogs, and poultry was immediately banned.

President Norsman established a Department of Sustainable Food and Fiber Production, whose major responsibility was to encourage and assist people who wanted to return to the land and farm on small acreages, especially those farmers who wished to follow sustainable agricultural practices.

Immediately after the federal Department of Lifelong Learning and Society was established, the department's secretary appointed a special commission charged with "taking the best from our educational past and integrating it with a new approach to lifelong learning." A preliminary report from the commission included recommendations to create tax-supported Community Learning Centers, or CLCs, throughout the country. Former for-profit schools closed as new taxing structures came into effect. The goal of the community learning centers was to provide learning opportunities for all ages, from the very youngest to the most elderly—what the commission referred to as "the circle of learning." These community learning centers were staffed by full-time, university-prepared, licensed professional teachers, experts in their subject matter areas as well as proficient in the best teaching practices for the age group with which they worked.

Once learners achieved basic literacy skills, such as reading, mathematics, and writing, they were encouraged to supplement their interaction with professional teachers by learning on their own, as well as learning in collaboration with others. The long-term goal was to teach everyone to learn how to learn. With that basic skill, learners could greatly increase their knowledge both with and beyond professional assistance. A central theme of the Department of Lifelong Learning and Society was "every person a teacher, every person a learner," which meant that everyone, not just those trained and licensed as teachers, was to be encouraged to share what they knew with others. For instance, a group of young people and older adults might work together to produce a play that would be performed at a learning center's theater. Or a group of older people and younger learners might work together to plan and then take a wilderness canoe camping trip.

The Town of Crystal River was one of the first to develop a comprehensive CLC. The center, located in a large building near the river, was shaped like a spiderweb, with the core area devoted to the Athenaeum. The Athenaeum included books, computers, a simulated space station, and various research materials available to the students attending classes at the learning center. The Athenaeum was also available to all the citizens of Crystal River, of New Start, and of the surrounding area. The auditorium, located next to the Athenaeum, not only was a place where plays and musical events were performed but also served as a virtual travel theater providing virtual trips to such places as the South Pole, the Sahara Desert, a Native American settlement in Alaska, and much more.

A recent brochure described the programs available at the Crystal River CLC:

> The Crystal River Community Learning Center provides learning opportunities, many of them hands on, for all citizens in the area, from the youngest to the oldest.

The CRCLC building includes the following learning areas:

Einstein Area: Creative thinking strategies for finding answers to tough questions.

Socrates Area: Critical thinking approaches for analyzing and interpreting research results, essays, reports, digital newspaper articles, editorials—all communications.

Jefferson Area: A vegetable garden where students learn basic gardening skills and grow vegetables for the center's kitchen.

Euclid Area: Learning to use mathematics, from the most basic to the most advanced.

Leopold Area: An outdoor nature area devoted to helping students understand the relationship of the environment to society by having hands-on experiences in the out-of-doors, including participating in an ongoing environmental research program, which the center sponsors.

Toni Morrison Area: Focuses on learning communication skills, with emphasis on clear writing as well as how to write personal stories and develop public speaking skills.

Frederick Jackson Turner Area: Where studying history can lead to a better understanding of people, places, and societal changes over time.

Mozart Area: Devoted to helping learners appreciate and participate in musical activities.

Georgia O'Keeffe Area: Hands-on experience with various art forms, including sketching, painting, photography, ceramics, video art, and filmmaking.

Marie Curie Area: Health education including nutrition studies, brain/memory research, and disease prevention. Area features an exercise room.

Champlain Area: Learning about local and global geography.

Karl Marx Area: Examination of social systems and understanding societal movements.

George Washington Carver Area: Learning about engineering and science. Hands-on approaches include participation in the center's ongoing science research projects.

One of President Norsman's first actions was to eliminate the national Office for Social Responsibility and cut off all funding to the handful of state OSRs that remained. Since the Eagle Party had suspended the US Constitution, President Norsman and Congress quickly reinstated it. Norsman also appointed a national Constitution Committee charged with bringing the Constitution up to date to fit the conditions of the present time as well as look forward to the future. Norsman, who had supported and continued to support the efforts of the Oldster organization, appointed several Oldster representatives, including Liz Carall, to the Constitution Committee. The president was aware of the various lists of rules, rights, and responsibilities that the Oldsters used in developing their now fifty-plus model rural villages in troubled parts of the country. Many of these new villages were modeled after the village of New Start. The president wanted to make sure that the rules, rights, and responsibilities lists that the Oldsters developed were considered in any revisions of the Constitution.

Norsman appointed a special banking commission to reinstate the dollar, but all transactions continued to be carried out electronically, thus saving on the printing of money. He insisted that the commission include the barter bank idea in their new model. Congress also voted to restore the Gregorian calendar and eliminate the Eagle Era calendar.

Meanwhile, the village of New Start continued to flourish, serving as a model for the similar rural communities that emerged across the country. The Onthaway Learning Center, with a new large log building, held workshops for Oldsters who came for training in everything from how to do sustainable agriculture to how to square dance, write poetry, and learn to play an instrument.

The tornado that killed Joe Vogel completely destroyed Sully Sorenson's bottling plant. Sorenson, with far more lucrative investments in New York City, chose not to rebuild the bottling plant, and deeded ownership of the park to the village of New Start. Everyone was pleased to see the Crystal River return to its former level after the flood and the bubbling spring once again fed the river.

A plaque was placed on the wall alongside the door leading into the New Start Community Learning Center, the former park headquarters building. It read:

In Memory of Joe Vogel,
Oldster member and untiring volunteer,
who helped make New Start what it is today.

After the elimination of the Office for Social Responsibility, drones no longer flew overhead, checking on what everyone was doing. The two big factory farms closed. In their place, several small family farms emerged. For health care, residents of New Start and Crystal River formed a cooperative hospital and a cooperative living center for those who could no longer work or volunteer their services. The living center encouraged younger and older people to live together in the same building, and in doing so, also share their talents and skills with each other. Every community now had a modern, tax-supported police and fire department, and everyone had affordable health care.

Upon the reorganization of Badger State University as a teaching, research, and outreach institution, Patrick immediately enrolled in the school's newly formed degree program, which combined face-to-face teaching with virtual learning experiences available on his digital all-purpose communication device. He completed his degree with a major in electronic journalism. Patrick's tuition was paid by the Oldsters as a way of thanking him for his help while they were struggling to establish the village of New Start. After graduation, Patrick returned to Crystal River and married Marilyn Barnes, who had been editor of the *New Start News*. Together they published the digital *Central Wisconsin Reporter*, which was one of the hands-on projects of the Toni Morrison Communication Area at the learning center. Students there worked as reporters and organized the layout for digital newspapers, which included area news and students' creative writing, artwork, photographs, and videos.

Liz's work on the national Constitution Committee took up much of her time for a year. Andy's brother, Herman, stayed on with Liz and Andy and helped them with the farm work. Andy was instrumental in helping organize the Central Wisconsin Vegetable Growers Cooperative, and he continued to volunteer to keep the Town of Crystal River beautiful with his flowers.

Liz remained president of the Crystal River Oldsters, which began meeting in a large room in the former Office for Social Responsibility building. Their numbers increased to include several people who lived in the village of New Start.

John Owens opened a digital communication shop in Crystal River, repairing electronic and other digital communication and entertainment devices. He looked forward to selling the shop to his employees so he could resume retirement.

Overjoyed with the success of the Church of Hope in New Start, Pastor Larry held services in a newly constructed church building in Crystal River. It was extremely popular. The building was shared space for Christians, Jews, Muslims, and any other group that wanted to worship there, as practicing religion was once again not only lawful, but also encouraged throughout the country.

Pastor Larry helped several of the fifty-plus model communities establish their own Churches of Hope. Part of his work—he said he would never retire—was training leaders for these Churches of Hope at the Onthaway Learning Center in New Start.

Still mourning the death of Joe Vogel, Emily Taylor taught creative writing at the Crystal River Community Learning Center and volunteered at the center's Athenaeum three days a week.

Liz and Andy Schmidt sat on their porch at sunset feeling the gentle evening breeze and listening to the sounds of the evening. A mourning dove called in the distance. Its melodious sound echoed down the valley where the Crystal River now flowed clear and clean.

"Did you hear what I just heard?" Liz asked.

"Yup, I heard the mourning dove."

"No, isn't that thunder I hear, way off to the west?" Liz said.

"By golly, you're right," Andy responded. "I hear it now, too. Nothing is as cold as thunder. Wonder what this storm will bring?"

Acknowledgments

~~~~~~

As is true for each of my books, many people helped me with this one, from developing the original idea (my son, Steve), creating the story (my daughter, Sue), to reading and commenting on innumerable early drafts (my wife, Ruth). A huge thank you to each of them.

I am also immensely indebted to the University of Wisconsin Press, including Director Dennis Lloyd and Executive Editor Raphael Kadushin, for their support of my work, especially my novels, of which this is number seven. Much thanks also to Communications Director Sheila Leary and Sales and Marketing Director Andrea Christofferson.

A huge thank you to several editors who helped make my sometimes tangled prose readable. They included Kate Thompson, who helped with the plot and character development; Michelle Wing, who helped straighten out the story line and corrected many little errors that appeared here and there in the manuscript; plus Managing Editor Adam Mehring and Senior Editor Sheila McMahon at the press, who supervised revisions.

Books by Jerry Apps

Fiction

The Travels of Increase Joseph
In a Pickle
Blue Shadows Farm
Cranberry Red
Tamarack River Ghost
The Great Sand Fracas of Ames County
Cold as Thunder

Nonfiction

Problems in Continuing Education
Improving Practice in Continuing Education
Higher Education in a Learning Society
Mastering the Teaching of Adults
Teaching from the Heart
Leadership for the Emerging Age
Telling Your Story
The Land Still Lives
Barns of Wisconsin
Mills of Wisconsin
Humor from the Country
Breweries of Wisconsin
One-Room Country Schools
Rural Wisdom
Cheese: The Making of a Wisconsin Tradition
When Chores Were Done
Ringlingville USA
Every Farm Tells a Story
Country Ways and Country Days
Living a Country Year
Old Farm: A History
Horse-Drawn Days: A Century of Farming with Horses
Garden Wisdom: Lessons Learned From 60 Years of Gardening
The Quiet Season
Limping Through Life: A Farm Boy's Polio Memoir
Whispers and Shadows
The People Came First: The History of Wisconsin Cooperative Extension
Wisconsin Agriculture: A History

Roshara Journal: Four Seasons, Fifty Years and 120 Acres
Campfires and Loon Calls
Never Curse the Rain
Old Farm Country Cookbook
Once a Professor

Children and Young Adult Books
Stormy
Eat Rutabagas
Letters from Hillside Farm (fiction)
Casper Jaggi: Master Cheese Maker
Tents, Tigers and the Ringling Brothers